S0-EAY-441

SHE WAS THE FIRST STOP ON A TRAIL THAT LED TO TROUBLE . . .

Breathlessly Vida gasped, "I wondered how long you were going to make me keep hinting. You knew I was inviting you from the very first minute, didn't you?"

"Maybe not right off. I caught on after a little while, though," Foxx allowed.

Vida's hand was trailing Foxx's forearm.

"Do you always expect a woman to make the first advances?" she asked.

"Not always. But with a lady like you . . ."

"Lady be damned! All of us are just women, when we need a man!"

MORE EXCITING WESTERN ADVENTURES FROM DELL

FOXX!

Zack Tyler

A DELL BOOK

Published by
Dell Publishing Co., Inc.
1 Dag Hammarskjold Plaza
New York, New York 10017

Copyright © 1981 by Zack Tyler

All rights reserved. No part of this book may be
reproduced or transmitted in any form or by any
means, electronic or mechanical, including photocopying,
recording or by any information storage and retrieval
system, without the written permission of the Publisher,
except where permitted by law.

Dell ® TM 681510, Dell Publishing Co., Inc.

ISBN: 0-440-12742-4

Printed in the United States of America

First printing—January 1981

FOXX!

CHAPTER 1

Foxx jumped, even though the train was still moving too fast to make jumping safe. He landed upright, feeling his boots sink calf-deep into the boggy soil. He bought time with a pair of quick shots into the oak motte that hid the unseen sniper, then for the risky moment needed to free his feet, he was exposed.

Whoever the unknown gunman was, his slow reactions saved Foxx. Just as he freed his boots and fell forward, a slug from the grove whistled over his head. Fighting the mucky, clinging soil Foxx fired again as he rolled to one side. He moved an instant before the sniper's next shot sent up a clod of wet earth from the center of the depression that marked the spot where he'd landed.

In the clear night sky the full moon was almost daylight bright, but even the brightest moonlight shrouds distant details instead of revealing them. To Foxx the dozen or so live oak trees that formed the motte looked like black blobs. He'd seen the muzzle flashes sent out by the hidden shooter's rifle, but couldn't spot their exact location among the trees. He sent another random shot into the motte, more to give the sniper something to think about than with any hope of scoring a hit.

There was no natural cover that Foxx could reach quickly. Construction gangs had ripped out all the trees along the right of way to make space for the gravel fill needed to support tracks in the boggy ground. A small pile of unused gravel, no more than a foot high, was the nearest thing to protection Foxx saw when he looked around.

Letting off another shot into the grove to discourage the concealed rifleman from taking careful aim, he crouched and ran for the gravel pile. Still another shot from the motte plucked at the dirt a few inches behind him, but by then Foxx had dropped behind the low heap of pebbles and was reasonably safe. His breathing returned to normal during the few moments he spent breaking the action of his American Model Smith & Wesson and thumbing fresh cartridges into the chamber.

Those moments spent reloading also gave Foxx time to take stock of his situation. He'd jumped from the caboose only a few seconds after the bobtail train, engine, and caboose had overrun the dynamite caps on the track that had caused the engineer to apply the brakes. The bobtail was far down the tracks, just beginning to back up.

With his eyes Foxx measured the distance to the oak motte; it was a good hundred and fifty yards from the pile of gravel. His hunter instinct told him the sniper hidden in the oak motte wasn't going to stay there the rest of the night. His detective experience told him that the sniper must have some connection with the case that had developed so unexpectedly just a few hours ago. He wanted to get his hands on the sniper before the gunman disappeared, and there was only one way to do it.

Foxx stood up. Offering himself as a target was a

gamble, but the sniper hadn't shown himself to be that much of a marksman. As he stood, Foxx spent another shell, firing at the motte. He moved as he shot, zigzagging across the boggy ground in the nearest thing to a run he could manage on that treacherous footing. Muzzle-blast spurted orange from the oaks, and a bullet zipped by his face with an angry buzz, missing him by inches.

Foxx was already moving toward the motte when the gunman fired. Although he couldn't see the hidden sniper, he knew the other man could see him closing the range. Foxx held his fire, but no more shots came from the motte. Foxx soon learned why. Hoofbeats muffled into whispers by the soft ground sounded from the clump of live oaks.

Straining his eyes Foxx tried to get a glimpse of the sniper, but the low-hanging foliage of the oaks cut off his view. He stopped, revolver ready in case the sniper planned to circle the trees and press his attack, but the gunman had given up. The hoofbeats faded into silence.

A toot from the locomotive broke the hush. Foxx turned to look. The accommodation train was backing up. Foxx took his time walking back to the track and waited until the caboose came to a stop in front of him. The lantern in the cupola had been relighted, he noticed; they'd doused it when the sniper's first shots had thudded into the caboose wall.

Halloran, Norton, and Mullins, the brakemen on the special, piled out of the rear door. They stopped in a huddle on the rear platform, squinting into the darkness. All three carried rifles. Before they could start down the steps, Foxx stopped them.

"You men might as well go back inside," he told them. "You won't find nobody to shoot at, now."

"Where'd they go?" Halloran demanded belligerently.

"There wasn't but one man. He got away on horseback," Foxx told them. Swinging up to the caboose step, he held the handrail and leaned back to call to the engineer, "You can highball again! The excitement's over!" A pair of short whistle blasts acknowledged Foxx's order and the accommodation train moved slowly forward.

"Ain't we going to try to track whoever was shooting at us?" Norton asked.

"In the dark?" Foxx asked quietly. "Him on a horse and us on foot?"

"Hell, it's almost daylight-bright out there," Norton said.

"Almost is a long way from there being light enough to see tracks," Foxx pointed out. "Anyhow, my job's up ahead at the trestle, not running after a man that's long gone by now."

Reluctantly the three brakemen trooped back into the caboose as the accommodation picked up speed. They stopped in the center of the bay. Mullins asked Foxx, "You wasn't hit, was you?"

"No. Shooting by moonlight's a tricky thing, Mullins. Hard to hold a target in your sights unless you've done a lot of it."

"You get a look at whoever was doing it?" Halloran asked.

Foxx shook his head. "He kept the trees between us. And a lot of the time I was rolling in the dirt, dodging his lead." He looked down at his clothes. Black peat-soil, as dark as the fabric of the suit, clung in small blobs here and there. Foxx shrugged. "It'll brush clean when it dries." He sat down, snapped open the cartridge-pouch sewed to his pistol belt, and replaced the shells he'd fired with fresh ones.

"Looks like you think there's going to be more trouble up ahead," Mullins suggested.

"I'd be a damn fool if there was and I wasn't ready." Foxx made the remark so casual that Mullins couldn't take offense. Then he added, "I don't look for shooting trouble. It's like I said a while ago—this has got the look of a one-man job. Chances are when I catch up to whoever set the dynamite, it'll be somebody carrying a grudge against the C and K, or maybe just mad at any railroad that's handy." He indicated the rifles the brakemen still held. "You can put 'em away. It's my guess the shooting's over for tonight."

"Suppose that fellow circled ahead of us to the trestle, how about that?" Halloran demanded. "For all we know, he's laying in another bunch of trees up there, waiting for us."

Foxx cocked his head and cupped an ear to indicate he was listening to the clicks of the wheels over the rails as the train picked up speed. "You figure he can move faster'n we are?"

"Maybe not," Halloran admitted somewhat sheepishly.

"Just the same, we'll feel better if we don't lock the guns up again," Norton said. "If we need 'em, we'd sure waste a lot of time getting 'em out again."

"Suit yourself," Foxx replied. "Now I'm going to lay down here on one of these bunks and catch forty winks. You men know what a callboy can do to bust up a fellow's beauty sleep."

Foxx stretched out on the bunk and closed his eyes. Several hours earlier he'd said good-bye to sleep for that night when the callboy had knocked at the door of his two-room suite in the Cosmopolitan Hotel. A quick waker, Foxx had tossed aside the light blanket he'd pulled over him when the fog began creeping in from San Francisco Bay into the open windows of his bedroom.

"Who is it?" he'd asked, knowing the answer before his hand found the robe that lay handy in the chair by the bed.

"Callboy, Mr. Foxx."

"Just a minute."

Foxx belted the robe around his waist as he padded barefoot into the suite's sitting room, which was bathed in the dim glow of a night-light burning beside the hall door. Experienced railroaders in the 1870's generally burned a night-light. The knocking of a callboy during the dark hours was never wished for, but always to be expected.

Knowing what he'd see, Foxx opened the door. He'd often wondered why the young sons of railroaders killed or crippled on the job almost invariably accepted the callboy jobs the railroad offered them.

There were a few old callboys, former trainmen too old or too crippled to keep working, and Foxx could understand why they clung to the only association most of them had ever known. They'd have been lost away from the hot-oil smell of the roundhouse and shop, or the sound of locomotive whistles wailing lonely in the night.

This was one of the young callboys, fresh-cheeked and wide-eyed in spite of the hour. "Mr. Flaherty said call you, Mr. Foxx," the boy said. "It's dynamite on the San Joaquin delta trackage in Solano County."

"You mean an explosion?"

"Oh, no, sir. It's not that bad. Some sticks of dynamite an old hobo found at the west end of trestle seven. He roused the section foreman, and the foreman wired Mr. Flaherty."

Foxx frowned. The California & Kansas Railroad had only a short stretch of trackage through Solano County, on the eastern route from Oakland to Sacramento. He couldn't pinpoint the location of trestle seven precisely, but knew within a mile or so where it was.

He asked, "How long ago did he find the dynamite?"

"Whillikers, Mr. Foxx, I don't know. I guess the dispatcher didn't find out. I don't s'pose it's been very long. Maybe an hour or two."

While he and the callboy talked, Foxx had made his decision. Sending the boy to rouse one of the four railroad detectives who worked out of the headquarters office in San Francisco would mean a delay of two or three hours in starting an investigation, and besides, Foxx had been deskbound for almost a month. He was tired of shuffling papers and reading reports.

"I guess the dispatcher redballed the section?"

"Yessir."

"All right. You go by the downtown depot and tell the dispatcher to order me up a bobtail out of the East Bay yards. I want it ready to go the minute I step off the ferry."

"Yessir. I'll be there in five minutes."

Glancing at the big Railroad Regulator clock on the wall, the only item that seemed out of place in the spartanly furnished room, Foxx went on, "I've got twenty-five minutes to make the one o'clock ferry, but to be safe, have the dispatcher wire the slip to hold the boat until I get on board."

"Yessir, Mr. Foxx. Is that all?"

"Yes. No—wait a minute. How'd you get to the hotel?"

"I rode my bicycle, Mr. Foxx."

"Good. On your way back to the roundhouse, flag down the first hack you see and tell the hackman to get over here and wait for me. If you don't run into a cab on the street, swing by the Palace Hotel. There's always a nighthawk or two at the stand in front of it."

"I'll find one," the callboy promised. "Anything else you want me to do?"

"No. Get cracking, now. I don't want to miss that ferry."

Foxx headed back to the bedroom. During the three years he'd headed the detective division of the C&K's railroad police, he'd answered too many after-midnight calls to waste time or motion on this one.

Passing through the bedroom he picked up a short, twisted stogie from the half-dozen that lay loose on the dresser and put a match to it. He tossed his robe on a chair and went into the bathroom. He stopped at the toilet long enough to drain the night's early accumulation from his bladder, then moved to the mirror beside the bathtub and examined his face. Rubbing a hand over cheeks and jaws, he decided shaving would be an unnecessary waste of time.

A spectator looking over Foxx's shoulder might not have agreed with the no-shave decision, for a blue-black stubble was already visible on his cleft chin and on his cheeks. Foxx did not bow to fashionable foibles, including the current one that dictated beards for men. He was clean shaven and kept his sideburns trimmed flat instead of combing them out with pomatum to fluff out stiffly from his face. Nor did he anoint his hair with macassar oil, though it lay in glossy waves above his high forehead and glistened as though it had been oiled. Below unusually heavy brows Foxx's eyes were brown, his nose crag-sharp between high cheekbones, his lips generously full. His chin was square, and his lean jawbone ran back to lumps of muscle below the clipped sideburns.

As Foxx moved to the washbasin and turned on the cold-water tap, he walked springily on the balls of his feet. The long sinews in his calves and thighs were ridged in well-rounded symmetry. His belly and chest, deceptively flat and smooth until he began to move, rippled into washboard layers as he bent over the basin and began to splash cold water over his face. His shoulders were broad, angling down in round cords under which the muscles stretched to meet the husky bulges of his biceps and forearms.

Foxx was not a hairy man. His skin was smooth except for the black mat of curls on chest, armpits, and pubis, but here and there the skin's smoothness was

broken by puckered scars that told of old bullet
wounds, by a few thin white weals marking healed
knife slashes, and by one or two jaggedly irregular
scars that gave no clue as to their cause.

Applying the rough towel vigorously, Foxx rubbed
his face and torso dry and went back to the bedroom.
He stepped into a fresh front-buttoned linen singlet,
chose a clean white shirt from the bureau drawer and
slid his arms into it. He'd picked a shirt that was free
of fashionable ruffles and buttoned instead of being
closed with studs.

Foxx's profession dictated inconspicuous clothing;
all his suits were either brown or black and tailored
of the finest English woolen broadcloth. He pulled
the oldest of his black suits off its hanger, and while
stepping into the trousers gazed frowningly at the
three rows of calf-high boots that stood neatly aligned
on the closet floor.

Foxx admitted readily that boots were his weakness
and that he indulged himself in buying fancy foot-
wear. The boots lined up in front of him were the
handwork of bootmakers from the many places his
railroad job and the travels that had preceded it had
taken him.

There were boots by Luchesse of San Antonio,
McCurran of Denver, Simpkins of Cheyenne, Pleas of
Tucson, Donaldson of El Paso, Christians of San
Francisco, Justin of Fort Worth, Craig of Bozeman,
Ezzard of Pendleton, Graves of Magdalena, and a
number of others. There were boots of brown leather
and tan, black and russet; boots with stitched designs,
with varicolored patterns of inlaid leathers, with high
heels and low.

In the end he chose a pair of plain-toed cavalry
boots, black instead of the army's regulation cordovan, but with the standard low cavalry heel. He
hitched up his trouser legs and sat on the side of the
bed while he pulled on white lisle socks, then he

stamped into the boots and twitched his trouser legs down over them.

Before donning his coat and vest Foxx lifted his holstered .44 caliber American Model Smith & Wesson from the bureau drawer and buckled on the gunbelt. He wore the revolver on his left side, waist high, the butt forward. There was no need for him to check the weapon's condition; Foxx scrupulously kept the tools of his trade in good shape. Shrugging into his vest and coat he reached instinctively for the .44 caliber Colt House revolver that was his backup gun, then changed his mind, and closed the drawer. There was no reason, Foxx told himself, to load his pocket with a short-range weapon; C&K cabooses all carried a rack of rifles and shotguns as standard equipment.

A four-wheel hack was waiting in front of the Cosmopolitan Hotel, and it got Foxx to the ferry slip with five minutes to spare before the Oakland ferry chugged out of its slip. While the broad-beamed side-wheeler churned across the choppy waters of the bay, Foxx ate a belated midnight supper or an extremely early breakfast; more as a precaution to stave off future hunger than because he needed food at the moment. In his experience cases that began after midnight had a way of dragging on until midnight the next day without time to pause for a meal.

He'd finished eating in time to be first in line to disembark when the ferryboat settled to a quivering halt in the slip at Oakland. The C&K's East Bay shops were a five-minute walk, and Foxx strode briskly through the cool, salt-tinged breeze. The bobtail he'd ordered was chugging on a siding, locomotive, tender, and caboose. A thin trickle of smoke wisping from the engine's stack told him that steam was up and the accommodation ready to roll. Anderson, the night superintendent, was standing beside the tender talking to the engineer. The two broke off their conversation when they saw him.

"Foxx," Anderson said. The engineer dipped his head in silent greeting. Foxx acknowledged both men with a nod. Anderson went on, "Dispatcher told me to ask you how long you figure the Solano line's got to show a red board. Says he's got to send train orders to the Limited before it pulls out of Sacramento."

"I sure as hell won't know that until I get to trestle seven and see what's happening," Foxx replied. "Tell him I'll get word to him as soon as I find out myself." He turned to the engineer and asked, "Are we ready to roll?"

"Whenever you say, Mr. Foxx."

"Let's highball, then."

Foxx waited until the engineer climbed into the cab and set the drivers rolling before he swung aboard the caboose. A trio of sleepy-eyed brakemen sat in the center of the car, one on a chair, the others on the facing benches that ran around the bay which extended beyond the caboose's sides. They nodded to Foxx with a mixture of respect and resentment showing on their faces.

He hadn't expected anything else. On any railroad brakemen and men from the detective force got along with what was at best an uneasy truce. Detectives generally blamed brakies for failing to keep a lookout sharp enough to prevent boxcar burglaries, and there was further resentment on the part of the brakemen because the detectives wore suits and white collars and rode the cushions instead of having to cling to the outsides of the cars in all kinds of weather, under all kinds of conditions.

Rightly or wrongly Foxx sensed a special grouch against him because he was railroad brass. He was one of fewer than a dozen men on the entire C&K system who could order up a special train at any time, and who could issue orders binding on any of the road's employees without going through channels. The authority his job carried earned him the brakies' respect, but because that authority often dragged them from warm beds at odd hours after too little sleep, it carried a residue of resentment with it.

Foxx accepted the resentment as a fact of life, ignored it as long as it didn't lead to disobedience. He used the respect as a lever to get things done fast and in the way he wanted them done. He returned the brakies' silent greetings with a hand gesture and sat down on the bench in the opposite bay. The man in the chair gave Foxx time to light the twisted stogie he produced from his vest pocket before swinging his chair around on one leg to face the detective chief.

"We all know who you are, Foxx," he began. "I don't guess you know us shacks, though. I'm Tom Halloran, he's Mullins, and that's Fred Norton. What we'd like to know is what's going to happen up the line where we're headed."

"I'd like to know that myself," Foxx replied evenly. "Maybe trouble, maybe nothing."

"We heard the super say something about dynamite," Norton put in. He made a question of his remark.

"That's right," Foxx agreed. "But I don't know for sure."

"If you're looking for there to be trouble, we want you to let us open the gun locker," Halloran said. He looked suggestively at the holstered revolver Foxx had revealed when he pulled his coat open to sit down.

"We'll wait to see if we need the guns, Halloran," Foxx said curtly. "There's no hurry."

His short reply discouraged further conversation, as Foxx had intended it to. After a short awkward pause the brakemen began talking among themselves, the kind of gossip common to men who work together as a unit day after day, the chummy conversation that shuts outsiders away from a group without its members appearing to be openly unfriendly. They ignored Foxx while the accommodation wound around the bay through the darkness, skirting the Berkeley hills, and highballed on the short straight stretch of track to Carquinez Straits, where the railroad ferry waited.

There were jobs for the brakemen at the crossing; they left the caboose to carry them out. After the ferry had carried the bobtail across the swirling waters where the currents of the Sacramento and San Joaquin rivers pushed through Suisun Bay to San Francisco Bay, the brakies came back into the caboose. Foxx could tell at a glance that they had something more than work on their minds.

Halloran planted himself in front of Foxx, legs astraddle. "We talked things over while we was on the ferry," he announced. "It ain't too far to trestle seven now, and for all we know there might be a gang of train robbers laying there waiting for the Limited to pile up when that dynamite blows. You know damned well they'll have guns and be ready to use 'em. If there's going to be shooting, us men wants to shoot back, or damned well know why not."

"So you want me to give you permission to open up the gun locker," Foxx said.

Mullins said, "Goddamn right we do! Train orders says you're in charge of this bobtail, so we're putting it to you fair and square."

"Yeah," Halloran added. "Man to man."

"I'll give it back to you the same way," Foxx told them. "I don't know, and neither does anybody else, whether that dynamite was planted by train robbers or some damn fool with a grudge. I will promise you this. If it's a gang, you'll get guns, but you won't use 'em until I say so. Is that fair enough to suit you?"

Silence hung in the air for a moment before Halloran said, "I guess that's all the answer we're going to get. How about it, boys? You satisfied?"

"Suits me," Mullins agreed.

"Yeah," Norton said. "Me, too." Then he said to Foxx, "We didn't set out to break operating rules, Mr. Foxx. We just don't want to wind up being sitting ducks."

"No more do I," Foxx answered. "Now let's put out the lantern in here so we won't be sitting ducks just in case there's somebody lurking along the right of way. I'll ask you to keep a close lookout on both sides of the track from now until we get to trestle seven. Once we're closer, we'll find out soon enough what's waiting for us."

During the next quarter-hour there was silence in the darkened caboose as Foxx and the brakemen scanned the passing landscape. The late summer moon bathed the flat swale through which the tracks ran in a silver glow. Here and there pools of standing water threw back little patches of brilliance as bright as the moon. Except for scattered live-oak mottes the land was flat and featureless. There was no sign of movement anywhere.

"Hadn't we oughta be getting close to trestle seven pretty soon?" Foxx threw the question out into the dark caboose.

"Pretty close," Halloran replied. "But it's on the east side of the section, and we ain't passed the section marker yet."

A staccato popping from beneath the train punctuated the brakeman's words.

"Torpedoes," Mullins said. "That was four of 'em, too. The hogger's gonna have to grab the Johnson bar real quick."

Four signal torpedoes on the track was the universal railroad signal for an engineer to bring his train to an emergency stop. The bobtail had been rolling up track since crossing the ferry, but now a squeal of steel on steel sounded as the brakes were applied.

Foxx stood up. He said, "I'll be first out."

Two long strides took him to the back door of the caboose. He was stepping onto the platform when Halloran exclaimed, "Hell! Them wasn't torpedoes, they wasn't loud enough! Them was dynamite caps we popped!"

Before Foxx could call a warning, one of the brakemen struck a match. Its flare gleamed through the caboose windows and silhouetted Foxx on the platform. A rifle barked from an oak motte and a slug tore into the wooden wall of the caboose. A second shot followed the first, ripping through the wall.

Though the train was slowing, it wouldn't come to a full stop for another quarter-mile. Foxx had seen only one thing to do. That was when he'd set his jaw and jumped off the platform.

CHAPTER 2

Foxx was roused from his light slumber by a prolonged series of whistle blasts. He sat up.

Halloran said, "That's the hoghead blowing the trestle."

As Foxx climbed up into the cupola to get a better view, the accommodation slowed to a crawl. Ahead, lanterns shone along the right of way. Foxx could see men standing beside the track, and one of them began waving a red lantern. Beyond the men Foxx saw the bog that trestle seven spanned, black wet soil that glistened in the twin glares of the moonlight and the locomotive's headlight. At the edges of the bog, he saw live-oak clumps. Foxx felt better when he saw how far away the trees were from the tracks. At least they wouldn't have to worry about being snipers' targets here on the trestle.

With a final harsh rasp of brakes the train stopped. Foxx climbed down from the cupola and went outside. The brakemen were already on the ground, rifles in hand, peering into the darkness.

A man wearing overalls stepped out of the group beside the tracks. He asked, "Mr. Foxx?"

"Right here," Foxx replied.

"I'm Ed O'Neil, the section foreman. And damn glad to hand this mess over to you. I hope you know something about dynamite."

"You mean the stuff's still out on that trestle?" Foxx stared at the young section foreman. "Don't you men on the work gangs know how to handle explosives?"

"Not my gang. Why would we, Mr. Foxx? Dynamite's used by construction crews, not just laborers like I've got in my gang. All we do is keep the track in shape."

"Looks as though I've been going on the wrong assumption," Foxx said thoughtfully. "I run into a lot of section gangs, and most of them have a man or two on them who used to be with a construction crew. I suppose I thought all section gangs did." He pushed his low-crowned black Homburg up off his forehead. "Well. It's up to me, I guess, to see what I can do, even if I'm not a dynamite expert. Where is it? At this end of the trestle?"

"About fifty feet out, over that big pond," O'Neil replied. He hesitated a moment and asked, "You want me to go with you?"

Foxx shook his head. "Not unless you feel called on to volunteer. I don't see that the job'll take more than one man. I'll need a lantern, though. And if that stuff's only fifty feet away, you'd better have your men pull back, and tell the engineer to back the train off, too."

"I'll take care of it," O'Neil said. "Anything else?"

"Yes. While everybody's moving back, I want to talk to the fellow who found the dynamite. A hobo, according to the report I got."

"Sure. He's sitting over there on the handcar. He didn't like the idea of sticking around, but I persuaded him to."

Foxx caught a note of hesitancy in the section foreman's voice. "I get the idea you might've had to do some pretty forceful persuading."

"Well—I might've been out of line, Mr. Foxx, but I dropped a sorta hint that the C&K might give him a few bucks for stopping to report what he'd found. He didn't have to come by the section house and tell me, you know; he could've just kept on going."

"Don't worry. I'll see that he gets something. I want to talk to him alone, though. You keep one of your men with you, and when I've finished talking with the fellow the three of you can ride the handcar back to where it'll be safe."

Carrying the lantern O'Neil handed him, Foxx walked over to the handcar where the hobo was sitting slumped down, looking as though he was half asleep.

"My name's Foxx," he told the man. "I'm head of the C&K's detective force." He paused, but the hobo made no reply. Foxx took out a stogie; as an afterthought he pulled out another and offered it to the bindlestiff.

"What in hell's that?" the hobo asked, peering at the black twisted cylinder.

"It's a cigar. Take it."

"By God, I've seen boes snipe butts outa the gutter that looked better'n that one. Anyways, I don't smoke no more. Keep your funny-lookin' cigar, mister."

"Suit yourself," Foxx shrugged. He lighted his own cigar and asked, "You don't mind telling me your name, do you? I've got to call you something, if we're going to talk."

"I didn't promise that O'Neil fellow I'd talk to nobody. Looka here, mister, I didn't hurt your damn tracks none just by walking along 'em. Sure, maybe I was figuring on hoppin' the first freight I could grab onto, but you can't prove that."

Hearing the reedy quality of the hobo's voice, Foxx frowned. He held the lantern up for a better look at the man, and saw the marks of age under the thick coating of grime on his face. The hobo was typical of the many of his kind Foxx had seen hanging about the railroad yards in scores of different places. He wore a shapeless felt hat, its brim warped and its edges ragged. His coat was too large for his scrawny shoulders, and the sleeves came down almost to his fingertips. A bandanna knotted around his neck served as collar and necktie. His trousers were baggy, his shoes cracked and scuffed. At his feet lay a small bundle tied in a big bandanna, the bandanna's ends knotted around a short stick—the man's bindle, as his kind called the bundle that contained their possessions.

Foxx said, "Look here, I'm not a yard bull. It's not my job to throw free riders off our trains or chase them off the right of way. Now, this business with the dynamite is pretty serious, and I've got to find out all I can about it. All I'm asking you to do is talk to me a few minutes. Nothing's going to happen to you if you tell me how you came to find that stuff on the tracks. In fact, if you feel like helping me, there'll be a nice piece of change in it for you."

"What the hell do I need with a wad of cash?" the hobo demanded. "Shit, mister, I've had money in my life, lots of times. All I do when I get flush is to go out and get boozed up and spend all I got. Then I go make some more so I can booze up again and spend that. Leastways, that's how I used to do. Now I don't even bother, and I get along pretty good. You give me money, I'll booze and blow it, then I'll be right back where I am now."

"What do you want, then? Or need? Clothes? A job?"

"You really mean you wanna give me something?"

"Anything within reason. You've saved the railroad a bad time, a lot of trouble, and you've saved some lives, too. We've got good reasons to be grateful to you, and the only way I can think of to show it is to give you a reward of some kind."

"By God, Foxx, you sound like you mean that!" For the first time, the hobo responded with a show of interest.

"I do. Just tell me what you need."

"Aw, shit! You'd just laugh at me if I told you what I'd like to have."

"No. I won't laugh," Foxx promised. "Go ahead. Tell me."

For a moment, the hobo studied Foxx's face. Then he said, "You know what I really want? I want a pass on your damned railroad. Good for me to ride the freight cars anyplace I wanna go, any time I feel like traveling."

Foxx fought down the impulse to laugh. The hobo was totally serious. He said, "I'll do better than that. I'll give you a lifetime pass to ride the cushions."

"Like hell you will! No, sir! None of your damned passengers cars for me! I don't wanna be stared at like I'm a freak. I want a pass that's good on freights."

"If that's what you want, I'll see you get it. But you'll have to tell me your name, so I can put it on the pass. And I'll add to the pass a free ticket to be in our yards anywhere you might be. That'll save you the trouble of chasing down a freight."

"Ah hell, I can get in and outa your yards without no bother." The hobo thought for a moment. "But if it'll keep your shacks and yard bulls off my neck, I'll take you up on that, too."

"You'll have both of them, then," Foxx agreed. "Now, let's get down to business on this dynamite that you've said is out on that trestle. But tell me your name, first."

"Joe."

"Joe what?"

"Ain't Joe enough? Shit, I been goin' along with just one name so long I'd feel uncomfortable trying to think what my real last name used to be."

"I guess Joe's good enough, then." Foxx smiled inwardly. He and the hobo had one thing in common, at least. Somewhere along the path to growing up, he'd mislaid his first name. Nobody called him anything but Foxx now. There were even times when he had to think hard himself to remember that his parents had christened him Samuel. He remembered the name the Comanches had given him better than the one his parents had bestowed, but that was neither here nor there. Better push memories aside and pay attention to the job he was here to do. He asked, "How'd you happen to find the dynamite, Joe?"

"Well," the old man began. He hesitated, then asked, "You wouldn't happen to be toting a bottle, would you? A drink sure would go down good right now."

"Sorry," Foxx told him. "I guess you've heard about Rule G, Joe?"

"Oh, shit. That. Sure, but I never figured anybody'd be fool enough to abide by it."

Rule G in all railroads' books of standing rules for employees forbade drinking while on duty or carrying a bottle of liquor while on the job. The penalty was being fired on the spot.

Foxx said, "I take my drinks when I'm off duty, like all railroaders do, Joe. And I'm on duty now."

"Well, hell, I guess it won't hurt me to wait. Let's see, you was asking—"

"How you found the dynamite."

"Sure." Joe heaved a sigh and took a deep breath. "It was like this. I was walking along the tracks, minding my own business. You wanna know the truth, I was looking for a jungle that used to be around here, where I'd find a fire and spend the night. It seemed to me, as best I recall, the jungle was at the other end of the trestle. Well, I'd just stepped out on the trestle and I see that black sorta heap right in between the rails. I guess I thought somebody'd dropped a overcoat, or something. I was right up on it before I seen it was a man laying there. I—well, I'll tell you the truth, Foxx, it spooked me at first for a minute. I figured it was some poor damn bindlestiff like me that'd fell offen a freight and got hisself killed. Right then, I felt mighty bad; yessir, Foxx, real bad."

Joe paused, sighed with the memory of his wasted sympathy, and when Foxx said nothing, went on, "When I see what I'd figured was a dead man jump up and come running at me, well, I don't mind telling you the truth, man to man. I was so scared I damn near shit my britches. But I held on to myself, and yelled at him, something about me just being a brother of the road, not a railroad bull, trying not to spook him back. But he didn't pay me no mind. He come on at me, and first thing I know, he was all over me, banging at me with his fists. I had my bindle on a stick, you know how we carry 'em I guess, and I tried to whop him with it, but he knocked it outa my hands and it fell offen the trestle. All I did was knock his hat off. And then he kicked me in the nuts, and while I was doubled up, hurting like hell, he knocked me offen the damn trestle."

"Wait a minute," Foxx interrupted. "If you knocked off this man's hat, you must've seen his face pretty clearly, bright as the moon is tonight."

"Oh, sure, I got a good gander at him, before he knocked me off of the trestle."

"What'd he look like? Can you describe him for me?"

"Big man, I'd say. Not as big as you, but big. Needed a shave as bad as I do." Joe paused to run a grimed hand over the inch-long stubble on his face. Then he went on, "Well, he had one of them kind of noses—hell, all I ever heard 'em called is Tennessee noses. You know, they start up between a man's eyes and run right straight down to his mouth. You know what I'm talking about, Foxx?"

"I know the kind of nose you mean." Foxx nodded. "What about the rest of his face?"

"Sorta long, I guess. High in the cheeks, hard jaw sticking out, measly little mean-looking mouth. Tip of his nose flared out damn near as wide as his mouth was." Joe stopped and shook his head. "I guess that's about all I recall."

"What kind of clothes did he have on?" Foxx prodded.

"I sure didn't pay no mind to what he was wearing. Pants and a shirt and coat, that's all I could say." Joe's forehead wrinkled under the tattered brim of his pushed-up hat, and he added, "Boots. He was wearing high-heeled boots, I'd bet, the way they thunked on the ties when he run offen the trestle. I recall now, that's what I thought at the time. High-heeled boots is all that'll make that kind of noise." The old hobo stopped and heaved a deep sigh. "That satisfy you good enough, Foxx?"

"Almost. But you haven't told me yet how you happened to see the dynamite."

"Oh. That. Well, sir, there I was in the goddam bog, wet as a scoured hen and just about as dead. Had to pull myself outa that mud by holdin' on to the ends of the ties. And I see them two little bits of something shining, right there in front of me on the rail. Like snake's eyes, they was. You ever seen the mean little shiny eyes on a copperhead, Foxx?"

"A few times," Foxx replied. "I think I know what you mean."

"You see eyes like them, you ain't gonna forget 'em, ever. Anyways, I kep' lookin', and right soon I could tell them things was copper, pushed into blasting fuse. Well, sir, I worked around hardrock mining country one time when I was younger, so when I knowed I was lookin' at blasting caps and fuse, I begun trying to find the dynamite, and there it was up under a tie, lashed on with some rope. Now, I been hoboing long enough to know dynamite on a railroad track means somebody's tryin' to blow up a train, and I didn't want no dead people on my soul, so I walked on up the track to the section gang house and told 'em. And that's the God's truth of what happened."

"You've earned your pass on the C&K, Joe. If you'll ride back to San Francisco with me after this is over, I'll see that you get it, and something more besides."

Joe chuckled. "You know what I'm gonna do, Foxx? I'm gonna hang around a railroad yard until a shack or yard bull calls at me, and I'm gonna let 'em cuss me good; then I'm gonna pull out my pass and show 'em. By God, I'll have me a time! Never thought I'd be able to hang something on a yard bull!"

"You wait around," Foxx told the old bindlestiff. "I've got to go out on the trestle and take that dynamite away. Then we'll go into town, and I'll see that you get fixed up."

"Be careful, now," Joe cautioned Foxx. "This deal's just between me and you right now, and if anything happens to you, I'm up shit crick without no paddle. Not no boat, neither."

Lantern in hand, Foxx walked out onto the trestle, his eyes glued to the ties. Just as Joe had told him, he saw the glint of metal on one rail, and when he got closer, the rope wrapped around the center of a tie. He reached the tie to which the dynamite sticks were lashed and set the lantern down. Kneeling beside it, he studied the layout.

To Foxx, the little rounds of copper did not look like snake's eyes. He saw them for what they were, blasting caps pushed into the hollow core of short lengths of fuse. The caps on the rail, when crushed

by the wheel of a locomotive, would spurt enough
flaming sparks to ignite the fuse, which in turn would
set off the dynamite. Foxx had been around enough
track-laying gangs to learn something about blasting.
He'd talked to powdermen, and seen some with a finger or two missing, or part of a hand blown away, by
the premature explosion of blasting caps. He knew
the fulminate of mercury in the caps was unpredict-
ably unstable, had heard stories of caps being set off
with a feather-light touch, or just by the heat of a
man's hand.

Fishing out his pocketknife, Foxx opened the large
blade. Very gingerly he severed the rope holding the
capped fuse cords to the rail. The stiff cords sprung
up wirily and quivered gently, the caps waving bright
in the moonlight, a lethal jigging.

Moving as though he was picking up an egg that
already had a cracked shell, Foxx gathered the fuse
cords into one hand and held them steady while he
sawed through them. He breathed more easily as soon
as they parted; there was now no way that the caps
could set off the dynamite if they should go off. After
that, it was easy to cut the rope lashing the dynamite
to the tie.

Walking softly, the lantern bail hooked in the
crook of one elbow, the capped fuse ends in one hand
and the dynamite in the other, Foxx stepped from tie
to tie, heading for the train.

O'Neil and one of the men from his crew, pumping
the handcar, reached Foxx ahead of the accommodation train. The section foreman was grinning broadly.
He indicated the dynamite and said, "We can all
breathe easier now."

"Not quite yet. That trestle has to be walked to
make sure there's not another bundle of dynamite tied
somewhere else."

"I hadn't thought of that." O'Neil frowned, then

said, "Sounds like a job I can handle. I'll take it on, if you want me to."

"Go ahead," Foxx nodded. "Wave if you find anything. I'll be watching; you wave me a signal if you find anything. If the trestle's clear, you and your crew can go on to the section house and tell the signalman to clear the block, and we'll head back to Oakland."

"And your job'll be finished," O'Neil said.

"No. That's where you're wrong. My job's just starting. This case won't be finished until I've hunted down the man who set this dynamite and put him behind bars. Because as long as he's loose, he's sure to try again."

CHAPTER 3

Looking at his surroundings, Foxx couldn't keep from contrasting them with the dirty, dreary peat bog he'd left just before sunrise that morning.

Gaslight diffused through the gemlike stained glass of Louis Tiffany's chandeliers was caught by genuine jewels in the tiaras, necklaces, bracelets, and rings of satin-gowned women and by the diamond shirt studs affected by more than half the men in the huge high-ceilinged room. Although almost eighty guests were present, the vast main salon of Caleb Petersen's Nob Hill mansion did not seem crowded. Liveried servants circulated among the guests, carrying silver trays laden with champagne flutes of the finest Baccarat crystal. Luminously glowing Oriental rugs covered most of the polished oak floor and trapped the voices of the guests, subduing what would otherwise have been an unbearable echoing of incessant laughter and chatter.

Foxx stood at one side of the room, watching the ebb and flow of movement with an impassive face. Like the other men, he wore evening clothes, though the studs in his stiff linen shirtfront were onyx rather than gold. His perfectly creased trousers concealed

Foxx's secret; instead of the conventional patent leather pumps considered requisite for a gentleman's evening dress, Foxx had on one of the gems of his boot collection, a pair of completely unadorned calf-high patent leather boots, made to his order by Worley of Cheyenne.

He noticed Caleb Petersen, president of the California and Kansas, moving through the shifting groups in the center of the room. Petersen was all smiles, obviously enjoying himself. But then, Foxx thought, old Caleb always did have a good time at this annual dinner which he hosted for the C&K's top executives.

There were other familiar faces in the crowd shifting around the room. Foxx saw his boss, Jim Flaherty, the head of the C&K police forces throughout the entire system, talking to Jared Blossom, the road's executive vice-president, near the center of the room. As his eyes flicked around the salon, he also noticed Nat Green, one of the men of his detective division, standing unobtrusively behind an arrangement of potted palms. Unlike Foxx, Green wore a dinner jacket; he would not be at the dinner table, he was there as a guard, not a guest. Two or three of the gangs from the notorious Barbary Coast had recently become active again, and there had been two cases of armed raids on dinner parties in recent months.

Foxx edged along the wall, avoiding the crowded center of the room, to where Green stood.

"Everything's quiet so far," Green said as Foxx came up to him.

"Let's keep it that way. There's enough jewelry in this place tonight to tempt a bunch of crooks to stage another raid," Foxx replied.

"Anything new on the dynamiter?" Green asked.

"No. My bet is that he'll try again, though. That kind usually does. I've sent a wire to all telegraph stations in the system to keep a special lookout on the trackage. Trouble is, there's just too many miles for us to cover, with the men we've got."

"Maybe. But I'd feel better if he was locked up right now, instead of roving free."

Foxx turned his attention back to the salon. Clara Petersen had just joined her husband, and was whispering in his ear. Foxx saw Caleb nod, then start looking around the salon. Must be getting close to dinnertime, Foxx thought. He moved away from Green, still keeping himself aloof from the crowd.

Petersen saw Foxx standing isolated from the crowd and began working his way to the wall where the detective chief stood. Foxx sipped his champagne and waited for the railroad's president to join him.

After a brief formal handshake, Petersen said, "Jim Flaherty tells me you saved us from what might have been a real disaster last night. There'll be some extra stock shares added to your bonus for that job, Foxx."

"Thank you," Foxx replied. "I hope Tom didn't magnify the case too much. It's still not closed, you know."

"So he said. Naturally, we're all concerned that the man who placed the dynamite got away. But I'm sure you'll find him and deal with him before he has a chance to try again."

Petersen turned to place his empty glass on a tray presented by a servant and he lifted a freshly filled one. He raised his thin arched eyebrows at Foxx, who shook his head. Caleb sipped the wine appreciatively, his eyes roving over the rooms.

While Petersen's attention was focused on his guests, Foxx covertly studied the man who had circumvented the behind-scenes maneuvering of the Big Four—Stanford, Hopkins, Huntington, and Crocker—and had more than met the efforts of the Central Pacific to stifle the growth of the California and Kansas. When the CP had refused to consider a shared-trackage arrangement on their line that spanned the Sierra

Nevadas, Petersen had uncovered an alternative route east. The C&K rails had been laid north from Sacramento up a river valley, across a pass in the Sierra's spine in a hairpin curve that opened the way down the eastern flank of the mountains onto the plains of Nevada Territory. When the Four had cut off the C&K's sources of California financing, Petersen had found elsewhere the huge amounts of capital necessary to push C&K trackage north and east into territory the CP had not yet reached to exploit.

Foxx grinned to himself as he looked at the C&K's president surveying the big room. Petersen was a man of imposing girth, and lacked by only an inch or so the height to carry his impressive stomach. His cheeks, above a square-cut and rapidly graying beard, were cherub pink, his eyes a guileless baby blue. Foxx had seen those eyes become both coldly menacing and craftily calculating. He knew their apparent innocence belied the sharpness of the brain behind Caleb's towering unwrinkled forehead. Petersen's hair, carefully pomaded and arranged to hide his increasing baldness, still retained a tendency to curl into babylike ringlets. The sum of his appearance was both impressive and disarming, a fact which the railroad president knew and used to achieve his objectives.

"I'm glad you weren't too busy on that dynamiting matter to join us this evening," Caleb said as he returned his attention to Foxx. "Clara's paired you for dinner with her sister. Vida's been here just a short time, you know, and the mourning period for her late husband's just ended. This is really the first social event she's attended for a year, and Clara's hoping you'll have some of your famous yarns to tell her, to keep her amused during dinner."

"I'll do my best," Foxx replied. He noticed that Petersen's eyes had never really stopped scanning the salon, and learned the reason for his preoccupation when Petersen turned back to him.

"Ah, yes. There's Vida now, in the light blue, standing next to Clara. Come along, Foxx. I'll introduce you now, and perhaps you'll keep her company until dinner's announced."

"It'll be my pleasure," Foxx said, following Caleb through the constantly shifting guests. They reached the two women. Foxx made his salutation to Clara Petersen, who immediately began to praise him for his success in averting the potential explosion. He disclaimed credit with a shake of his head and a smile; looking at the woman in blue who stood beside Clara, he was thinking that his response to Caleb a few moments earlier might have held more truth than politeness.

Clara's sister looked nothing at all like Petersen's plump, matronly wife. She must, Foxx thought, be much younger than Clara, whose chubby face showed puckered wrinkles at the corners of her eyes and mouth, and folds of loose flesh at her throat. Foxx had no time to make a complete appraisal of his dinner partner, as Clara started to introduce them.

"Vida, dear, let me present Mr. Foxx. You heard Caleb and me praising him at breakfast."

Foxx made a proper bow over the gloved hand Mrs. Martin extended. "Caleb was telling me I have the honor of escorting you to dinner," he said. "I'm looking forward to your company, Mrs. Martin."

Vida Martin smiled, showing perfect and dazzlingly white teeth between lips so brilliantly red that Foxx wondered if she might not have touched them with a bit of rouge.

"No more than I am of yours, Mr. Foxx," she replied. "Clara and Caleb have spoken of you more often than at breakfast today. They've been tantalizing me with stories of your adventures ever since I got to

San Francisco. I'm sure we'll find a great deal to talk
about."

Before Foxx could make a suitable reply, the
muted musical quiver of a struck gong sang through
the salon and the guests began to move slowly toward
the tall double doors that opened at the end of the
salon. The Petersens made a hasty apology and hurried to the diningroom to greet the guests as they entered. Foxx and Mrs. Martin found themselves
surrounded by other guests, which made personal
conversation difficult. Foxx was kept busy returning
the greetings of executives from the C&K's San Francisco office, many of whom he saw only at rare inter-
vals.

He was not too preoccupied, though, to keep an
eye on his dinner partner, and more and more he
liked what he saw. Vida Martin was tall; the jeweled
aigrette in her upswept red hair was level with his
eyes. Like many red-haired women, Vida's skin was
extremely white, and as they passed under the glitter-
ing light of one of the chandeliers Foxx thought he
saw an almost invisible scatter of freckles across her
aquiline nose. Her lips, the feature of her face that
had first caught Foxx's eyes, pouted slightly above a
firmly rounded chin. Her eyes looked green in the
changing light between the chandeliers.

Foxx noticed also that she moved beside him with
an easy stride and that her body under the clinging
satin of her evening gown did not seem to be as rigid
or as perfectly cylindrical as did those of most of the
women who wore the full-length corsets that current
fashions dictated. Vida had a definite waistline and
stood erect without leaning slightly forward. In the
low V of her dress that looped down from a smoothly
rounded neck, he thought he could almost see her
breasts moving freely as she turned. For a moment
the thought passed through Foxx's mind that perhaps
she might not even be wearing a corset at all.

Then they were in the diningroom, actually the ballroom, which was being used because the mansion's diningroom could comfortably accommodate only fifty guests, and their attention was concentrated on finding their place cards. The cards were finally spotted, halfway down one side of the huge horseshoe-shaped table, and Foxx held Vida's chair while she took her place.

"Goodness!" she exclaimed, looking around the room after they both were seated, "I don't think I'd enjoy being in Clara's place. The consultations that she's been having all week with the caterer and her butler! I certainly wouldn't fit in very well as the wife of a railroad nabob!"

"She and Caleb both seem to enjoy it," Foxx commented.

"Yes. I suppose it's luck that they do. And Caleb does have a position in society to uphold."

"Which I'd say they do pretty well."

Foxx indicated the dozen black-coated waiters who were moving around the table, half of them placing individual portions of caviar on small service plates beside each diner, the other half following only moments behind with cups of clear consommé. Along the walls, busboys in short white jackets stood waiting to remove the caviar plates and soupbowls when they'd been emptied.

"Oh, yes, that's another thing, Mr. Foxx. Having all these servants underfoot. I know they're extra help, brought in by the caterer just for tonight, but I don't think I could get used to having to plan a dinner of this kind."

"Caleb said you've just moved to San Francisco, Mrs. Martin. If you intend to live here and move in the circles that he and your sister do, you'd better get used to big dinners and elaborate service. It's that kind of city." Foxx shifted slightly in his chair as the busboy came up to remove his caviar plate. He glanced up at the youth just as Vida Martin spoke.

"Perhaps I will, in time," she said. Then she saw Foxx's brows puckering and asked, "Is there something wrong?"

"No. I just thought I recognized that young man who took our plates away. I can't quite place his face, though."

"That's part of your job, isn't it? A part that you carry with you everywhere, remembering the faces of criminals?" Mrs. Martin shook her head. "With all the criminals abroad these days, I don't see how you can remember so many faces."

"I can't remember all of them," Foxx told her with characteristic candor. "I manage to keep a lot of faces in mind, but I don't think anybody can remember the faces of all the wanted men I'm likely to run across in C&K territory."

"From what Clara and Caleb were saying this morning, when they were talking about that terrible risk you took in removing the dynamite from that trestle, you must travel a great deal, Mr. Foxx. That must mean you enjoy it."

"Not all the time. I've kept on the move most of my life, though, and if I have to sit behind a desk too long I get to feeling cramped."

She returned to her previous remark. "Even if getting away from your desk means taking frightful risks, such as you did last night?" She pushed her soupbowl away.

"That doesn't happen every day, of course."

Foxx saw the busboy approaching to remove the soupbowl and concentrated on the youth's face. Some chord of memory was twanging in his mind, but he still couldn't associate the busboy with any of the "Wanted" fliers he'd seen.

He watched the young man's white-clad arm as it passed across Vida Martin's shoulder. He frowned again when he noticed the youth's hand removing the plate from the table. It was not the soft white hand of someone used to doing kitchen work. The busboy's hand was tanned and calloused; its creases and lines were etched with ingrained grime, the kind that is ground deeply into the skin itself. Foxx saw, too, that the little finger had been broken and set badly, so that it was permanently curved. Foxx had seen enough little fingers like that on the roping hands of cowpunchers to know that such a finger was almost a trademark of anyone who roped cattle.

Suddenly Foxx found the association he had been searching for. The busboy's nose started between his bushy eyebrows and ran down in a straight line to thin, flaring nostrils. He had a small mouth, high cheekbones, a prominent jaw, and a long face. In every detail, the busboy fitted the description given by Joe the hobo of the man who'd attacked him on the Solano trestle.

"Excuse me," Foxx said to Mrs. Martin.

Pushing back his chair, he started after the busboy. Foxx forced himself to move slowly; he wanted to avoid drawing the attention of the guests as well as his quarry. He looked at the corner where Nat Green was stationed. The railroad detective was sitting at a small table that had been placed behind the screen of potted palms. Foxx couldn't tell whether Green was watching the salon or eating his dinner.

Foxx glanced along the table. As far as he could tell, none of the diners had noticed his movements. He allowed himself to move just a little faster. The busboy was less than a dozen steps ahead of him now. Foxx slid a hand under the lapel of his tailcoat, reaching for the Colt House revolver that rested there in a specially tailored pocket holster. He brought the pistol's hammer back to half-cock, and with his middle finger revolved the cloverleaf-shaped cylinder a half turn. Before he could draw, the busboy looked over his shoulder and saw Foxx behind him.

Letting the tray he carried fall from his hands with a clatter of metal and a crash of broken china, the busboy began to run. Heads turned all along the table. The busboy turned, a stubby derringer in his hand. Foxx dived forward when he saw the gun. The busboy fired just as Foxx dropped. The slug from the derringer whistled harmlessly over Foxx's head and thunked into the wall at the back of the salon.

Foxx had dived ahead, but not far enough. The busboy was still out of reach, and in falling, Foxx had landed on his chest. His right hand, still closed on the Colt inside his coat, was trapped between his body and the floor. His left shoulder began throbbing, but he ignored it.

Before Foxx could roll to free his gun, the busboy swiveled and fired the derringer's second barrel at Caleb Petersen. Foxx was on his knees a split second after the second shot. He knew the busboy's derringer was useless now. Instead of shooting the youth, he called, "Get your hands up and stand still!"

With a defiant shout, the busboy turned and began running toward the salon's service door. Foxx saw Nat Green moving from the corner to cut the youth off, but he was closer than Green. Launching himself in a tremendous leap, Foxx again sailed through the air.

This time he hit the busboy while he was still sailing. The youth went down under the impact of Foxx's body. Foxx knocked the derringer out of the youth's hand and grabbed his wrist. He brought his captive's arm up and back. The busboy writhed with pain, but he was helpless. To save his arm, he turned over until he was facedown on the carpeted floor.

"Handcuff him!" Foxx snapped to Green.

There was no need for the command; Green was already searching for his handcuffs. The detective grasped the busboy's free wrist and snapped the cuff on it, then secured the wrist that Foxx was holding.

"What d'you want to do with him?" Green asked Foxx.

"Get him out of here fast! Into the kitchen. I'll smooth down the people in here."

All the guests were on their feet now, and several of the men were hurrying toward the spot where Foxx and Green were standing with the busboy. Foxx waved them back. All the men knew Foxx. They slowed their advance, stifled their questions, and started trickling back to the table. There was one exception. Jim Flaherty, Foxx's immediate superior, continued to join Foxx. Nat Green had already left with the captured busboy.

"What the hell happened?" Flaherty asked Foxx.

Foxx brought his hand up to pull a stogie out of his vest pocket before he remembered that he was carrying them in the tail pocket of his evening coat. He found the pocket's opening and lighted the stubby twisted cigar while he continued talking to Flaherty.

"I'm not sure yet, Jim. You know the description of the man the hobo caught setting the dynamite?" Flaherty nodded. Foxx went on. "Well, that busboy fits it to a tee. We might have lucked out. No way of knowing yet, not until I've asked him a lot of questions."

Caleb Petersen came up, hurrying to join them. "By God, Foxx, you just might've saved my life when you sailed into that fellow! Look here." He pointed to the left shoulder of his tailcoat. A tear showed in the fabric, bits of the horsehair shoulder padding sticking out of the rip. "He was after me, wasn't he?"

"Not much doubt about that," Foxx replied. "Lucky I was as close to him as I was."

"Luck, hell!" Caleb snorted. "I'd call it damned fine detective work. But no more than I'd expect from you." He looked around. "Where'd the son of a bitch go?"

"Nat Green's got him," Foxx said. "I'm going to question him, see what I can find out."

Flaherty said, "I'll go with you, Foxx. If we get at him quick, before he's had a lot of time to think about things, we'll have better luck." He turned to Petersen. "I hate to break up your dinner, Caleb, but this is more important than food."

"Why, you're not going to keep me from finishing out the party, Jim." Petersen grinned. "We'll just go right on eating, as soon as everybody gets over being excited. You and Foxx go on and question that man; I'd like to know why he tried to kill me. But when you've asked him all the questions you need to, come back and finish your meal. I don't intend to waste any of that fine food we've got waiting in the kitchen. I've got to pay for it anyhow, so we might as well enjoy it."

Foxx and Flaherty exchanged glances. Halloran said, "Damn it, Caleb, we can't question that fellow the way we need to in time to get back to the table before dinner's over."

"Now, you two listen to me," Petersen said. "Clara's been working for more than a week getting everything for this dinner just right. Why, we haven't even started to eat yet. There's Humboldt sole coming up next, then veal cutlets with creamed peas and mushrooms, and some real fine Smithfield ham; then there's a big cake for dessert. By the time we've had coffee and brandy, it'll be close to midnight. I'll just tell the caterer fellow to keep everything hot for you."

"Like Jim just said, it's likely to take us a while to get that young outlaw started talking," Foxx warned.

"Take as long as you need to," Petersen told them. "But I want both of you back here to finish dinner with us, and by God, men, that's an order!"

CHAPTER 4

As they walked to the kitchen, Jim Flaherty said to Foxx, "Caleb's really got a bee in his bonnet about us getting back to the dinner table. It's not like him. He's always been set on his men finishing up a job."

"How many times in his life you think Caleb's had a pistol slug come that close to him, Jim?"

Flaherty stared at Foxx for a moment, his face blank, then said, "Oh. Yes, that would be enough to upset a man like him. Caleb never heard a shot fired during the war. He served here in California with the militia. And he does his fighting with money and brains, not fists or guns."

"Does pretty well with both, too," Foxx chuckled. Then, in a serious voice, "He meant what he said about us coming back to finish dinner, though."

"Oh, I never did doubt that. Well, let's see what we run into before we start saying what we will or won't do."

Nat Green had immobilized the busboy by passing the youth's hands through the back slats of a heavy chair and handcuffing his wrists. The youth was sitting facing the back of the chair. He glared at Flaherty and Foxx when they came into the butler's pantry, which was the closest entry to the kitchen, but said nothing.

Green asked Foxx, "Don't you think I oughta go scout around the house a little bit, now you're here? There might be somebody with this little bastard."

Foxx inspected the handcuffs which held the busboy to the chair before answering, then turned to Green. "You think he's anchored here for a few minutes, Nat?"

"Sure oughta be. That chair's too heavy for him to drag very fast."

"Good. Let's step outside and talk a minute, then," Foxx suggested.

They went back into the diningroom. Most of the guests had returned to their seats by now, and Caleb Petersen was urging those still on their feet to sit down.

Foxx asked Green. "Did you question the busboy at all, Nat?"

"I didn't have time to ask him anything but his name. He just looked off past me like I hadn't said a word. You're going to have a time making him talk, Foxx."

"Did you search him, Nat?" Flaherty asked.

"Sure. Just as soon as I had him cuffed to the chair. There wasn't one damn thing in his pockets except a dollar or two, and these." Green dug two copper-jacketed cartridges out of his pocket and held them out in the palm of his hand for the others to see. "Forty-one caliber, for that derringer he used."

"No papers?" Foxx frowned.

"Not one damn thing but loose change and these slugs," Green repeated. "And like I said, he didn't pay no more attention to what I asked him than if I hadn't been there."

Flaherty said, "I imagine he'll get tired of keeping his mouth shut before we do of asking him questions."

"One thing I did do," Green added. "I asked that Armand fellow, the caterer or whatever he is. He said he never saw that busboy until about eight o'clock this morning, when he came around asking for a job. Armand needed extra help for tonight, so he hired him on."

Foxx frowned. "Eight o'clock? You sure of the time, Nat?"

"Sure I'm sure! That was about all Armand told me about the little bastard. Didn't know his name or anything else."

"All right, Nat," Foxx told the detective. "You go on and check around the house. Come on back here when you're finished. By that time maybe Jim and I will have decided what we want to do."

As Green left, Flaherty said to Foxx, "You seemed upset when Nat told you what time the busboy got back. Why?"

"Because if he was here in the City at eight o'clock"—Foxx frowned—"I know damned well he couldn't've set that dynamite in Solano County last night. I looked up the time when the signalman at the block beyond the trestle wired the dispatcher—it was exactly 10:48. And whoever'd put those dynamite sticks in place was still hanging around when I got there on the accommodation five hours later. It was a few minutes before four o'clock when we pulled up at the trestle, and the sniper and I had swapped shots about a half hour earlier."

"How does that prove anything?" Flaherty asked.

"Figure it out for yourself, Jim. There's no way in the world a man on horseback could get across the straits, or even on a ferry upriver, and ride clear across Contra Costa County and wind up in San Francisco much before noon."

Flaherty was thoughtfully silent for several minutes. Foxx knew that his chief was running over the timing in his mind. At last Flaherty said, "I guess you're right about the time."

"I know I'm right, Jim! Hell's bells, the engineer hogging that bobtail I rode was pushing it as fast as he could. I didn't get back to the city until after ten. Damn it! The busboy couldn't've planted the dynamite, even if he does fit the description Joe the hobo gave me of the fellow he caught planting the dynamite on the tracks."

"If it wasn't him, maybe it was his twin brother," Flaherty suggested with a humorless smile.

Foxx started to reply but stopped short, his mouth open. For a moment he was silent; then he said, "By God! I think you just hit the target, Jim! Brothers! Maybe not twins, but brothers or relatives of some kind. We're not after one man, we're looking for two!"

"No. We've got one of them, in the pantry there."

"And there's one still on the loose, if we're right. Well, that makes things look different. Let's go see if we're any better than Nat was at getting him to talk."

Foxx and Flaherty went back into the pantry. The busboy twisted around long enough to glare at them, then turned his head away and stared at the pantry wall.

Foxx walked around to face the youth. For a moment he studied the busboy's defiant face. The prisoner was older than he'd first thought, Foxx decided. He guessed the busboy's age as the early twenties. He said, "You might as well tell us your name. We'll find out, sooner or later, you know."

Involuntarily, the youth's mouth twitched as though he was about to speak. He caught himself in time. Then he turned his head far enough to one side to keep from looking at Foxx.

Flaherty moved over into the prisoner's field of vision. He said, "If you don't talk, your brother will.

He's facing a lot more serious charge than you are. All we can hold you on is attempted murder."

This time the busboy's mouth opened, but he stopped himself from speaking. He turned his head away from Flaherty and found that he was looking at Foxx. Still he stayed silent.

Foxx shifted his position, just as Flaherty had, to a spot where he again faced the prisoner. Now the busboy bowed his head to rest it on the back of the chair to which he was handcuffed.

Foxx questioned Flaherty with a look. Flaherty shook his head, then motioned to the pantry door and pressed a forefinger across his lips. Foxx nodded and tiptoed after Flaherty, through the door and out to the diningroom again.

When they'd silently closed the door, Flaherty said, "It looks like we've got a lot of softening up to do before we get that one to open his mouth."

"You're right," Foxx agreed. "I've seen his kind before."

"Do you think we can beat anything out of him?"

"I suppose we could," Foxx said thoughtfully. "I might have a better way than that, though. The trouble is, it'd take a little bit of time."

"How long?"

"Overnight, at least. Probably even longer."

"What's your plan?" Flaherty asked. "This is still your case, you know. I'm not going to tell you how to handle it."

"It'd be the first time in a long time, if you did." Foxx smiled, remembering.

When he'd first been given command of the C&K's detective division, Flaherty had looked over his shoulder almost constantly. Foxx had reined in his resentment until his temper snapped, and the blowup between the two had stopped just short of a fistfight. But after the dust had settled, Flaherty had stopped interfering and given Foxx a free hand, even though

the two were frequently at odds over Foxx's unortho-
dox methods.

Foxx went on, "If it's my case, I'll go about settling
it my own way, then. You go on back to the table and
sit down. I'll be along in a few minutes, as soon as
Nat reports back."

Flaherty bristled. "You mean—"

"I mean," Foxx broke in levelly, "that since you
just said you're not going to tell me how to handle
this, I'll do it the way I think is best."

Flaherty stared at Foxx angrily for a moment, then
shrugged. In a tight, clipped tone he said, "If that's
the way you want to do it, it's fine with me. When
you get something to report, let me know, if you feel
like it." His back angrily stiff, he stalked away.

Foxx watched his superior, a grin creeping slowly
over his face. He looked down at his evening suit, saw
dust on his coat lapels and trousers where he'd hit the
floor during the busboy's capture, and began brushing it away. His palm encountered the House Colt in
its tailored pocket and reminded him of something
else. He took the revolver out and pulled the hammer
to half-cock, then rotated the cloverleaf-shaped cylinder until one of the deep grooves between its four
chambers was directly under the backstrap. When he
lowered the hammer, the firing pin rested in the
groove between the top pair of chambers. In this
mode, the cylinder's side grooves were in line with
the top of the grip.

When Foxx restored the weapon to its pocket, the
bulge it made was so small it would escape the notice
of any but a very careful observer. Foxx had similar
holster pockets tailored into all his suits. There'd
been times when the little snubnosed House Colt—
called the Cloverleaf by some—had escaped a searcher
who'd removed the bulky forty-four from its holster.
On more than one occasion the backup gun had

saved Foxx's life, and it had gotten him out of bad scrapes too many times to count.

While his hands had been busy, Foxx's mind was also at work. He'd reached a decision regarding the prisoner's treatment while he and Flaherty were still in the pantry but hadn't been sure that his chief would give him a free hand in carrying it out. The exchange with Flaherty had settled that; now Foxx waited patiently for Green to return.

His wait was short. Green skirted the edge of the ballroom, where the guests had resumed their interrupted meal, and stopped in front of Foxx.

"Nothing wrong that I could see," Green said. "I even took a look outside, but there wasn't anybody there, either, as close as I could tell."

"I didn't think there would be. All right, Nat, I'm going to turn the busboy over to you."

"You mean you want me to take him to jail?"

"Good God, no! That's the last place I want him to be!"

Green's puzzlement showed in his worried frown. "What am I supposed to do then, Foxx? Keep him handcuffed and stay here watching him?"

"Not that, either, Nat. You know the old C&K stores building, out on Fremont?"

"Sure. I wasn't working for the road when they moved out of the old place, but before I was promoted to detective, when the C&K police was mostly Jim Flaherty and a half dozen more of us, I used to have to check on the old buildings regularly. Until everything but the warehouse was torn down, that is."

"That's where I want you to take the busboy. There's a little closet in that old building, right about where the chief storekeeper's office used to be. It hasn't any windows, and the door and walls were still stout the last time I was out there."

"You want me to lock up the busboy in that closet? Is that the idea?"

"Yep. Dig up a hasp lock for the door if you have to. I guess you'd better figure on standing guard the rest of the night, too."

"What about Caleb's shindig, here? Who's going to take over for me?"

"I imagine Jim and me can do that without too much trouble. Oh, yes. One more thing, Nat. Before you toss that busboy in the closet out there, strip him."

"Strip him? You mean take his clothes off?"

"You don't have to take 'em off him yourself. Make him do it. And put the cuffs back on when he's undressed. Except for them, I want him bare-ass naked. Don't overlook his shoes and socks, either. Don't feed him, don't let him have any water."

"Jesus, Foxx! You're being pretty rough on the youngster!"

"I intend to be. Don't waste any of your sympathy on that youngster, as you call him, Nat. He's not as young as he looks to be when you first see him. And you've found out how tough the little bastard is. And while you're watching that closet after you lock him up, don't answer him if he yells at you, don't make any noise he can hear."

Green shrugged. "I guess I don't see much reason for all of this, but you're the boss. I'll do just what you've told me to, Foxx."

"Good. Now, get going. I'll get there fairly early in the morning and relieve you."

Foxx watched Green enter the pantry, then turned his attention back to the dinner table. His own chair next to Vida Martin was the only one empty. At the head of the table, Caleb Petersen was holding the attention of those seated closest to him with a story of some kind. The waiters were bustling around, serving another course. Foxx suddenly realized that he was ravenously hungry. He gave his tailcoat and trousers a final brushing with his hands, then went and slid into the chair beside Vida Martin.

"I'm glad to see that you're not hurt, Mr. Foxx," she said, as Foxx took his crumpled napkin from the table and draped it across his lap.

"Sorry I had to leave without asking you to excuse me, but there wasn't time enough to be polite."

"But you did ask me," she reminded him. "Though, goodness knows, I wouldn't have taken time to be polite."

"Guess I forgot I'd asked, then. I knew I had to move fast. The busboy looked just like the description I'd had of the man who set that dynamite on a C&K trestle last night."

"Yes, Caleb made quite a speech about you. I'm surprised your ears weren't burning, the way he praised you."

"Maybe they did and I was just too busy to know about it."

A waiter serving the next course interrupted their talk. He set in front of them plates containing thick slices of richly pink ham swimming in a cherried sauce. Almost before the first waiter had left, a second appeared to refill their wineglasses. Foxx's hunger swept back over him. He could hardly wait for his table companion to take the first bite before digging into the dish himself. He ate as fast as he dared. When he'd swallowed the last tangy bite of the sauced ham, he looked around to see Vida Martin's eyes fixed on him.

"Sorry," he apologized. "All of sudden, I was about half starved."

"Small wonder." She smiled. "You'd just begun to eat when the excitement began, and you've certainly worked off the few bites you had a long time ago." She fell silent when a busboy appeared to remove their empty plates. When the boy had gone, she went on. "Tell me about your job, Mr. Foxx. Is it always as exciting and dangerous as it's been tonight?"

"Not a bit of it. I spend a lot more time than I like to think about sitting at a desk and going over reports."

"I think I'd prefer that to risking my life, the way I saw you doing earlier."

"Why, that—" Foxx stopped short. He'd been about to say that he'd gotten caught up in worse situations, which would have approached bragging, and he had no use for braggarts.

Before he'd framed a suitable answer, the arrival of the next course saved him. He looked at the plates that had been put before them, half a grilled prairie chicken accompanied by fat stalks of the asparagus that was just beginning to be cultivated under hot frames in the peat soil of San Joaquin County. He began scraping away the rich cream sauce that garnished the asparagus.

"I see you don't enjoy sauces," Vida commented.

"Oh, I like 'em all right. But if I ate every evening the way I am now, I'd be too fat to move around fast when I have to."

"You certainly moved fast enough a while ago, when you were after that busboy who tried to kill poor Caleb. Can you tell me who he was, and why he did that?"

"There's not anything to tell you right now. Not that I'm holding back—he just wouldn't say a word when we tried to question him. I don't know anything more than I did when I jumped the fellow."

"Caleb hinted that the shooting might have some connection with the dynamite setting. Is that right?"

"It might be. I've still got to make sure, though."

"I see." She looked at him for a moment before saying, "I hope you won't mind if I say something personal, Mr. Foxx, but it seems to me you're favoring your left arm a little bit. I heard the crash when you landed on the floor, and I don't see how you could have avoided getting hurt."

"I guess it jarred my shoulder a little bit," Foxx admitted. In truth, he'd forgotten about the shoulder until he'd sat down and begun eating. Now he raised his left arm experimentally and felt a twinge of pain. "I guess it's just beginning to stiffen up."

"What you need is to soak in a tub of hot, hot water while somebody massages that shoulder," Vida suggested. Then her eyes widened and she brought her hand up to cover her mouth. "Oh, dear! That was a very forward and unladylike thing for me to say, now wasn't it?"

"Not a bit," Foxx assured her. "I sure didn't take it that way."

"Well, if it was, I hope you'll forgive me. I've been a widow for only a little more than a year, and I've been alone most of the time. I'm sure I must've been thinking what I'd do for my husband, if he'd hurt himself the way you did."

"Why, that's only natural, seeing you were used to being married such a long time."

She frowned thoughtfully. "Not really a long time. I'm quite a bit younger than Clara, you know. Chester and I were married only eight years before he died."

"That's long enough to be used to having a husband to look after, I guess. But I don't mean to bring back sad memories for you, Mrs. Martin."

"Oh, I'm quite over the shock, now. And I'm sure moving to San Francisco will be good for me."

They finished the prairie chicken and were served the soufflé; almost immediately the cake followed, to bring dinner to a close. Clara Peterson stood up, the other ladies followed her example, and she led them into the salon, leaving the men in possession of the table.

While the busboys cleared the table, removed the

cloth, and set out the brandy, whiskey, and port de-
canters along with boxes of cigars and coffee cups,
Foxx found himself the center of attention. Though
Caleb Petersen hadn't hinted at a link between the
attempted dynamiting and murder attempts, the C&K
executives had quickly made the connection.

Jared Blossom, the road's executive vice-president,
exercised the privilege of rank by putting the first
question. "What about it, Foxx? Is there a gang after
us, or just one crazy man?"

"That's what I'm trying to find out now, Jared. Doing that's going to take more time than I've had,
though."

Blossom turned to Flaherty. "What do you think,
Jim? One man, or a gang?"

"You heard what Foxx says, Jared. It's his case. I'm
just standing by to give him whatever help he might
need."

Elbert Blenkinship, one of the C&K directors, said
to Flaherty, "What I can't understand is how this
man who tried to kill Caleb got in here at all. It
seems to me that you'd have had more than one man
on duty to make sure we were all safe. Why, that
maniac might've shot at any of us!"

" 'Tis an unfair question y've put tae Jim, Mr.
Blenkinship," put in Andrew MacPherson, the road's
mechanical superintendent. "Next, y'll be wanting tae
know why I didn't know a locomotive boiler was
gaeng tae blow up, or y'll be asking why he didn't
foretell a crop failure that reduced our freight
revenues."

Blenkinship thought about this for a moment, and
nodded slowly. "You're right, MacPherson. None of
us can see into the future yet."

"I'd better say something right now and get it off
my mind," Foxx said. "We'll find the answers as fast
as we can, but while we're looking, don't expect us to
pass on too much news until the case is closed.

There're always things that we don't want to talk about while we're digging into a case."

Caleb Petersen put an end to the discussion. "You know my rule at these dinners, no talk of C&K business. Let's sit down and enjoy ourselves now, until it's time to join the ladies."

Perhaps the flare of violence earlier had dampened the spirits of Caleb's guests. At previous annual dinners hosted by the Petersens, the C&K executives had dawdled for an hour or more after dinner, swapping jokes and trading personal experiences. Tonight, there were few jokes cracked, and scant laughter at those which were. Almost every man in the room seemed preoccupied and anxious for the affair to end. Caleb sensed the uneasiness and cut the afterdinner session short. They went into the salon, where a similarly subdued group of women waited for them.

Foxx saw Vida Martin standing alone a step or two behind Clara Petersen, who was talking with one of the guests. He went to bid his dinner companion good night.

"I've enjoyed the evening, too, Mr. Foxx, in spite of all the disturbance. I do hope your shoulder isn't too painful," she replied.

"It's nothing to worry about. Don't give it another thought."

Clara turned at that moment and saw Foxx and Vida. She said, "Oh, Mr. Foxx. I was hoping I'd see you before you left. You must know how grateful I am to you for saving Caleb's life tonight."

"I can't claim a great deal of credit for that, Mrs. Petersen. Derringers are notoriously inaccurate at the distance the shot was fired."

"Just the same, you were there to act, and you did act, very bravely." Clara turned to Vida. "Just as soon as the guests leave, I'll tell Bishop to have the stableman bring a carriage around for you, dear. But I do wish you'd change your mind and stay with Caleb and me tonight."

"No, Clara," Vida said firmly. "I don't want to be underfoot after you and Caleb have had such a trying evening. But don't worry about me, I'm not in any hurry to get home."

As Clara turned away to speak to another departing guest, Foxx said to Vida, "I thought you were staying with your sister."

"Oh, no. I've taken a flat on Pine Street near Larkin, until I can find a house I like. I value my freedom too much to want to stay here with Clara and Caleb, Mr. Foxx."

Foxx hesitated almost imperceptibly before offering, "I'll be honored to see you home, Mrs. Martin, if you don't mind riding in a livery hack. I ordered one to wait for me from ten o'clock on, and it should've been outside for the past hour."

"I don't at all object to riding in a livery hack, Mr. Foxx." Her green eyes looked directly into Foxx's brown ones as she went on, "And I'd be very pleased to have you see me home." Foxx wondered if he was misreading the message he thought he saw in Vida's eyes as she added, "Yes. Very pleased indeed."

CHAPTER 5

Vida Martin shivered under her fur coat and drew its collar higher around her throat as the livery hack turned off Pine Street into Larkin. A fog had drifted in from the Pacific during dinner, and she and Foxx looked out of the glassed carriage windows at a night shrouded in mystery. The gaslights on their iron standards along the street created blobs of luminous opalescence, but the carriage rolled through a shimmering and impenetrable veil.

She said, "I'm glad I put a lot of extra coal in my fireplace before I left this evening. Now I'll have a warm room to come back to."

"Sounds right nice," Fox commented. "I'm just as glad I won't have to be out much longer, too."

"I thought you were going to talk to the man who tried to shoot Caleb."

"Not until morning. I want to let him stew a while. He might open up easier after he's been locked up all night." Foxx didn't add that the busboy was shut up in a windowless closet, naked in its total darkness. He shifted his position on the leather carriage seat.

Vida asked, "Has this cold fog started your shoulder hurting?"

"Oh, maybe a little bit. Not enough to bother me."

"Do you think a warm toddy would ease the pain, Mr. Foxx?"

"I imagine it would. I'll make myself one before I go to bed."

"If you'd care to put off bedtime a while, I'll mix one for you," Vida offered.

"Now, that's a nice thing for you to do. I'll just accept your kind invitation, Mrs. Martin."

With a creaking of harness the carriage came to a stop. Foxx opened the door and took Vida's elbow as she stepped down to the curb. He told the hackman, "You'd better wait," and walked beside Vida to the door of the three-story brick building. She had her latchkey in her hand by the time they reached the door. In the hallway she indicated the stairs.

"My flat's on the second floor," she told Foxx, and as they climbed the stairs, added, "It's small, but I'm hoping to find a house before too long. One that I can manage with only one or two servants."

Entering the flat, Foxx's first thought was that compared to the unadorned simplicity of his two rooms in the Cosmopolitan Hotel, the flat was luxurious. Through the portieres of the inner door of the small foyer in which they stood, he got a glimpse of the living room, dimly lighted by an invisible lamp. Thick carpeting covered the floor; there was a mantelless fireplace with a bed of dying coals burning in its grate; a satin-upholstered divan stood on one side of the grate, a velvet-cushioned easy chair on the other. Bay windows, also draped in velvet, were on either side of the fireplace. Above the grate hung a portrait sketch in oil of a younger Vida Martin.

Foxx dropped his hat on a table beside the door before helping Vida out of her coat. A faint sensuous whiff of perfume warmed by her body wafted up as she drew her arms out of the sleeves. He laid the coat on a bench seat that stood beside the table and followed her into the living room.

"Do sit down, Mr. Foxx." Vida indicated the sofa. "I'll put on the kettle to heat the water for our toddies."

"Suppose I stir the fire and put on fresh coal while you're doing that."

Foxx went to the fireplace as Vida left the room. He broke the crusted slag that covered the coals in the grate before adding fresh lumps from the scuttle that stood on the hob. With his back to the room, he studied the portrait sketch while waiting for Vida to return.

Even in the dim light, the portrait dominated the room. It showed a face delicate but strong, and the unknown artist had caught a hidden sensuality in his limning of her lips that Foxx hadn't noticed in the woman who'd been his dinner companion. He was still looking at the painting when Vida spoke from behind him.

"It's not a completed picture of me, Mr. Foxx, but I like it. A young friend of Chester's family did it while we were in Nice shortly after we got married, a young art student named Sargent."

"I like it, too," Foxx said.

Vida came to stand beside him. He saw that she'd stopped between living room and kitchen long enough to remove her gloves and take the jeweled aigrette out of her upswept red hair. She'd also renewed her perfume; the heady scent wafted to his nostrils by the heat from the grate was much more pronounced than when he'd helped her out of her coat. The delicate skin of her arms gleamed like tinted porcelain in the firelight, and the glow of the newly replenished coals brought a blush of pink to her upturned face.

"That fire feels good," Vida said, extending her hands to the glow. "I suppose in time I'll get used to

San Francisco fogs, but the weather here's so different!"

"It takes a while," Foxx agreed. "I'm in and out of the city so much that I never quite get used to it, either."

"How does your shoulder feel now? Is the heat from the fireplace easing the pain?"

"Now, you're making too much of a to-do over that little bump I got," Foxx protested. "It's not all that bad."

"You oughtn't neglect it, though." Vida hesitated for a moment before suggesting, "Maybe—maybe if I rubbed the sore place a little bit? Or would you—well, would you think I'm being too forward?"

Foxx was not at all hesitant in replying. "Of course I wouldn't, if you think it'd help."

"It certainly won't do any harm. Here. You just take off your coat and vest and sit on the sofa. I'll stand behind you to rub."

Foxx laid his tailcoat and vest across the armchair and sat down where Vida had indicated. She'd already moved behind the sofa. She stroked his shoulder with her fingertips, tentatively at first, then began kneading vigorously.

Foxx was surprised at the strength in her fingertips. She kept up the massage, her hands dancing along his shoulder. One hand began moving further and further down his arm, rubbing his bulging biceps. Foxx heard her begin to breathe faster and looked up. Vida's eyes were closed dreamily. Her chin was tilted upward, her full red lips parted in a smile that showed her gleaming white teeth.

Foxx realized she'd reached the point where her coy pretense would soon vanish. He took the hand that was stroking his biceps and tugged gently. Vida opened her eyes, saw Foxx's face below her, and made no resistance as he pulled her arm until she leaned forward over the sofa. He held her there for a moment, until he felt her body's tension relaxing. Her free hand give up its massaging and she began to stroke Foxx's neck. Foxx twisted around and brought his lips up to meet hers.

Vida gasped. Her mouth opened and Foxx felt her tongue thrusting against his lips. He met it with his. They held the kiss until the strain of breathing became painful for both of them and Vida's arm was trembling in Foxx's hand. He released her wrist, but she made no effort to straighten up. In the plunging V of her dress front Foxx could see the white globes of her breasts trembling gently.

Breathlessly, Vida gasped, "I wondered how long you were going to make me keep hinting. You knew I was inviting you from the very first minute, didn't you?"

"Maybe not right off. I caught on after a little while, though."

Vida's hand was trailing Foxx's forearm. She let it fall to his crotch. Foxx was already half erect after that first lingering kiss, and the gentle pressure of her hand caressing him through the fabric of his trousers brought him more fully upright.

"Do you always expect a woman to make the first advances?" she asked.

"Not always. But with a lady like you—"

"Lady be damned! All of us are just women when we need a man!" Her hand closed around him. "And I'm finding out that you're pretty much a man right now." With a final squeeze she released Foxx and took his hand. Foxx stood up. He tried to take her in his arms, but Vida shook her head. "There's no use wasting time in here. The bedroom's warm by now."

Vida led Foxx down a short hallway, past an open door through which he glimpsed the kitchen. In the bedroom as in the living room a mantelless fireplace recessed in the wall radiated glowing warmth. The room was almost square, and most of its center was taken up by a double bed, the covers folded back neatly. A long narrow vanity-dresser stood along one wall; in the opposite wall a door to the bathroom stood ajar. Flocked wallpaper with narrow blue stripes covered the walls. The shades of the windows that opened on both sides of the bed were drawn tightly. A lamp on the vanity cast a soft light through its frosted chimney.

Vida said, "Would you like to undress me first, Foxx? And then I'll undress you. Or would you rather be first?"

"Whatever pleases you most, Vida."

"Me first, then. Oh, I'm not selfish, but I like to know a man's looking at me and getting harder by the minute while I'm taking off his clothes."

Vida turned her back to him and Foxx began fumbling with the line of buttons that ran from the neck of her dress to a few inches below her waist. The buttons were tiny, so small that Foxx fumbled with the first few for several minutes before he learned how to handle them with his big fingers. Vida did not try to hurry him. One of her hands had crept back to his crotch and she was feeling him again.

Foxx freed the last button. His fingers had told him as he worked down the back of the dress, freeing the buttons, that his guess at dinner had been right—Vida was not wearing a corset. He tugged the dress, and Vida helped by shrugging it off the shoulders. The dress fell around her feet. She slid a shoulder strap free, and aided by a gentle tug from Foxx her satin slip rippled to the floor atop the dress.

Foxx was completely hard by now. He rubbed his chin over Vida's bare shoulders, inhaling the perfumed fragrance that flowed from her soft white skin. Vida shuddered. She ripped at the buttons of her camisole, and it dropped. Foxx cupped her bared breasts in his hands and began to knead them gently while running his lips along her shoulders and neck.

Vida was quivering. Impatiently, she loosed the waistband of her knickers and kicked free of knickers, shoes, and stockings while Foxx was still engrossed in caressing her upper body.

"Hurry, Foxx!" she gasped. "I want you inside me right now!"

Twisting in his arms, Vida reached around his chest and began unbuttoning his evening shirt. She'd forgotten his bow tie, and tore it free, ripping his collar from its studs, then whipping off his shirt. She attacked the buttons of his linen singlet and pulled it down to his waist. Now they stood bare chest to naked breasts. Vida pulled Foxx to her and began twisting her body to rub the budded pink tips of her breasts raspingly against the wiry black curls of his chest.

Foxx sought her lips again and caught them in a kiss. He felt Vida's hands fumbling at his fly and the cloth of his trousers sliding down his legs. Vida grasped his erection and squeezed the hard fleshy cylinder. She turned her head to break their kiss.

"Hurry, Foxx!" she repeated. She took a step backward, pulling him with her toward the bed.

Foxx tried to kick free of his trousers and singlet, but the narrow legs of the trousers would not slip over his boots. Vida was tugging him harder and he almost lost his balance. He shuffled ahead a clumsy step, tripping on the folds of cloth that hampered his legs.

"I—I can't get out of my damn boots!" he muttered.

"I need you right now, Foxx!" she moaned. "Now!"

They'd almost reached the bed. Vida gave a final tug and pulled Foxx with her as she fell backward across the bed. She raised her legs and guided Foxx into her. He felt her hot wetness enclosing him. His feet still planted in a tangle of clothing on the floor, Foxx drove into her.

Vida moaned, a prolonged sobbing sigh. Her body shook as Foxx thrust again, and her moans became a succession of small screams that she stifled in her throat. Her body was writhing under Foxx now. He felt her heels digging into his back as she pulled her hips up to meet his strokes.

"Deeper, Foxx, deeper," she urged. "Oh, you don't know how good you feel to me!"

Her hips were jerking now, her neck arched back, buried in the soft mattress. Her hair had become loosened when she fell onto the bed and streamed in tendrils across her white shoulders.

Foxx was thrusting faster now, his face buried in Vida's soft shoulder, her perfume strong in his nostrils. Vida's movements under him became frantic. Her hands dug into Foxx's back as she began to jerk spasmodically.

"I can't wait for you, Foxx!" she gasped. "But don't stop!"

"Don't worry. I won't," Foxx promised.

He kept up the tempo of his deep steady strokes until he heard Vida sigh deeply and felt her body relax. Then he went into her deeply and lay quiet.

"I'm sorry I couldn't wait for you," she whispered. "But it's just been too long since I've had a man inside me. Can you stay hard a while longer?"

"Sure. Don't let that worry you." Foxx moved his feet, trying to get them untangled from his clothing.

Vida smiled, "I didn't do a very good job of undressing you, did I?" she asked him.

"It was my boots. They've got to come off before I can get my pants off."

"I'd finish the undressing now, but I don't want to let you go. I feel too good with you inside me, still so big and hard."

"I like the feeling as much as you do."

Foxx pressed even more strongly against her and Vida clenched her teeth on her lower lip as she closed her eyes and moaned with delight. Then she opened her eyes and looked at him questioningly.

"Can you stay hard while I get your boots off? And the rest of your clothes? I know you're uncomfortable."

"Don't worry about me, Vida. I'm just starting out."

"All right. As long as you're sure."

Foxx stood up. Vida patted his erection and stroked it lingeringly. Foxx managed to shuffle back a half step to give her room to slide off the bed. She stretched sinuously, her arms above her head bringing her breasts up, their pink rosettes still pebbled, darker tips tautly erect. Her body shimmered in the soft light, full high breasts, flat stomach, flaring hips. A tangle of curls as red as her streaming hair shone moistly gleaming in the V of her rounded thighs.

Foxx bent forward to caress her breasts with his lips, taking the tips into his mouth in turn and rasping across their pebbled stiffness with his tongue. Vida wrapped her arms around his head and pulled him to her tightly.

"Oh, Foxx!" she sighed, "I don't want you to stop, but you'd better, or I'll pull you down on the bed again, boots and all!"

Foxx released her. She looked at the floor, at the tangle of trousers and singlet that trapped his feet, the black patent leather tops of the boots rising from the folds of cloth.

"Oh, my!" Vida chuckled throatily. "What a mess! How on earth am I going to get your boots off?"

"Only one way I know, unless you've got a boot-jack."

"Which I don't."

"We'll have to take 'em off cowboy style, then."

Vida shook her head. "I don't understand."

"I'll show you."

Foxx hobbled to the foot of the bed and braced himself. He pulled up one trouser leg and raised his foot. Vida watched him, her eyes questioning. Foxx showed her how to straddle his calf, and smiled approvingly as she swung her leg over his, giving him a glimpse of pink nestled in a fringe of red. Her soft white buttocks bulged as she leaned forward. Foxx planted a foot on one side and pushed. The boot yielded, and a moment later so did the other one. Foxx stepped out of the tangle of trouser legs and singlet.

Vida dropped the second boot and turned to look at him. "Oh, how wonderful," she smiled. "Most men would be drooping by now."

"I don't lie unless I've got to," Foxx replied. "And if you're ready—"

"And I'm ready, too, even if I can't show it the way you do. Even readier than a minute ago." She held out her arms and Foxx stepped up to her. They sidled to the bed, tongues entwined in a kiss that was not interrupted even when she guided him into her and met his thrust as he entered. For a long moment Foxx did not move, then he felt Vida stirring beneath him and began a long steady stroking that he prolonged until Vida's head began tossing on the pillows, her red hair wreathing her face in a dancing nimbus of color as her back arced beneath his thrusts and her moans became a single wail of ecstasy that trailed off into breathless fulfillment.

Even then Foxx stayed hard and kept himself buried in her pulsing wetness while he continued to plunge into her. Vida began to respond once more, almost as quickly as she had before. Foxx felt himself building in response to her wordless urgings, the quickening of her breath on his shoulder, to the woman scent that now hung over them. Vida's soft cries became one long ecstatic ululation from deep in her throat. Foxx drove himself harder and plunged deeper until the moment came when he could no longer hold back and his hips jerked in quick involuntary jabs that matched Vida's sharp convulsive upthrusts. He let go then and felt himself jetting and gave way to exhaustion that left him sprawling on her still-twitching body.

Slowly they roused after long moments of satiated silence. Vida cradled Foxx's head between her hands and kissed him, a deep and satisfying kiss. "Thank you, Foxx," she whispered. "I guess you could tell how long I've had to wait."

"I'd say it's been a while."

"More than a year. And feeling like everybody was watching me. That's one reason I moved out here, as much a reason as thinking it'd be nice to live near Clara. And Chester was a good lover, Foxx, almost as satisfying as you are. But not as big or able to hold on as long." Vida pulled her head back and studied Foxx's tanned face. "Foxx," she repeated. "Isn't that funny. I don't even know your first name yet."

"There's not many who do. And nobody calls me by it."

"Not even your lady friends?"

"Not even them. And I hope you don't—"

"Feel jealous?" she broke in. "No. Not a bit. We're both grown up, Foxx. I promise you that I'll never be a bit jealous of you, and I won't expect you to be jealous if I look at somebody else."

"You've got a deal, Vida. Because I've never had a wife. The kind of hours I keep, getting roused up in the middle of the night to go out on a case, not knowing how long I'll have to be away—things like that make me pretty poor husband material. There's not many women who'd want to put up with a man they can't count on being around when he's needed."

"I get the idea you're not too interested in looking for a wife, anyhow," Vida smiled. "That suits me. I think I'd like to be free for a while myself. As long as you'll spend some of your free time with me now and then."

"Oh, you can count on that." Foxx reached out a hand and stroked it in a long caress from Vida's hips up over her smooth stomach and her breasts. She nestled up to him with a long contented sigh.

"You're an amazing man, Foxx. Tell me about yourself. What made you the way you are? Tell me why you wear patent leather boots with evening clothes instead of pumps, like other men do. Tell me about some of the people you've known. I'm curious. I've never met anybody like you."

Foxx shook his head. "That'd take too long. We haven't got that much time tonight. You'll find out about most of it, I guess, a little bit at a time. Don't forget, I got a new case on my hands, a prisoner waiting for me to question him."

"But you told me you wanted him to stay locked up all night."

"Sure, I do. But morning's going to get here a lot faster than I like to think about. And for all I know, you might be figuring on sending me home even before then."

Vida responded by pulling Foxx to her for a long kiss, which grew into a fevered embrace of thrusting tongues and stroking hands. He cupped her breasts in his palms and felt their tips grow firm under his fingers. Her warm soft hand crept down and encircled him, and his flaccidity swelled into firmness in response to her gently persistent squeezes. His quick response excited Vida even while she was arousing him. She threw a leg across his waist and began rubbing his tip across the warm silken skin of her inner thighs.

"You know where I want you to go home to," she whispered. "And we don't need to hurry too much. Daylight's not that close. We'll have plenty of time for more than just one encore."

CHAPTER 6

Foxx was wiping the last traces of lather off his face after a leisurely shave when a knock sounded on the door of his Cosmopolitan Hotel suite. He belted his robe around his waist and went through the bedroom and sitting room to open the door. Jim Flaherty was standing in the corridor. He came in, and Foxx closed the door.

"I guess you just got back from questioning that busboy," Flaherty said; it was both query and statement.

"No. I'm just getting ready to go do that now."

"And I suppose you haven't been to the office yet?"

"Why? Should I have? Did something else happen last night?"

"No. Except that I'll bet Caleb's walking around like a cat on a hot cookstove, waiting for you to report."

"I don't report to Caleb, Jim. I report to you."

"And I report to Caleb, damn it, and so will you if he wants you to!" Flaherty shot back. "I know him better than you do, Foxx. The dynamite alone would be enough to get him upset, but that was him the busboy tried to kill last night. I don't blame Caleb if he takes it pretty personal. I guess you would, too. I know damn well I'd want to know who it was tried to kill me."

"Caleb's just going to have to wait, then," Foxx told his chief.

"I thought you were going to question that little son of a bitch last night," Flaherty frowned. "What happened?"

"I don't recall saying anything about when I aimed to start asking questions," Foxx replied. He opened the humidor that sat on a low table beside an easy chair and took out a stogie. Lighting it would give him an excuse for not talking, and Flaherty needed a few minutes to cool down. He touched a match to the stogie. He told Flaherty, "I said it'd be a while before I questioned the busboy, but I didn't say how long."

"Why're you putting it off this way, Foxx?" Flaherty asked.

"Jim, that busboy's got to stew before he'll break down and talk. He's got to think about the ugly things we can do to him, and get hungry and thirsty. By the time his head and guts have hurt a while, he'll be ready to talk to me."

"That sounds to me like something pretty close to torture." Flaherty frowned.

Foxx snorted. "Torture, hell! I learned about torture from the Comanches when I was just a kid. Shit, Jim, I seen white men and red men both carved up and whittled away a little bit at a time. I'll torment that busboy, but I won't torture him."

"Simmer down, damn it," Flaherty interrupted. "Call it torment, then." He looked at Foxx curiously. "You know, Foxx, this is the first time I ever heard you say much about what you saw when you were with the redskins. I don't even know how long they had you."

"Hell, I don't either." Foxx's voice was sober. "It seemed a lot longer than it was, I guess. I used to puzzle it over in my mind a lot, years back. After a while it dawned on me it was gone and over, and how long it'd been didn't matter no more. But as close as I can tell, I was with the Comanches nine years or thereabouts. Now let's talk about something else."

"There's not much else to talk about until you get something out of that busboy."

"I'm glad you see that," Foxx said drily. Then he smiled. "It looks like you'll just have to smooth Caleb down until I get something to report."

Flaherty sighed. "I've done that enough times now so that my excuses keep getting thinner and thinner. You can be a real ornery son of a bitch when you want to, Foxx."

"Look who's talking!" Foxx grinned. Then, growing serious, he added, "I'm not going out of my way to be merciful, Jim. You saw how that fellow shut up tight as a clam last night. I'm softening him up the best way I know how."

"I know it. I was just hoping you'd have something."

"Give me a little while. I'm going out to talk to him now. Maybe I'll have something by this evening."

"Where're you holding him?" Flaherty asked, then quickly said, "No. Don't tell me. I don't want to know. I told you last night, it's your case to handle your own way. You would anyhow, of course."

"Of course," Foxx agreed, keeping his voice neutral and his face straight.

"I'll go along to the office, then, and try to keep out of Caleb's way until I hear from you."

When Flaherty had left, Foxx dressed slowly, thinking as he did so. It was the first chance he'd had to put his mind fully on the case since he'd left Vida Martin's flat two hours earlier. They'd dozed intermittently, never for more than a few minutes, until Vida had dropped into an exhausted sleep and Foxx had gathered up his clothes, dressed quietly in the living room, and let himself out. It wasn't until he'd gotten to the hotel that Foxx remembered he'd never gotten the toddy which had been Vida's ostensible reason for inviting him in.

After the bath and shave which Foxx had grown accustomed to accepting as a substitute for a full night's sleep, he began to plan his approach to the stubborn busboy. When he'd donned a fresh shirt and stepped into the trousers of the dark brown suit he'd decided to wear, Foxx had worked out a rough outline of his plan. He put the flesh on the outline while he was pulling on a pair of tan kangaroo-hide boots decorated with snakeskin inserts, and shrugged into his vest and coat. The Colt House revolver went into the holster pocket of the coat. Foxx was ready to face the day. Outside, the fog had blown away; the morning was bright and warm.

Hackneys were scarce at that hour. Foxx stood in front of the Cosmopolitan until he became impatient and decided to walk the three blocks up Bush to Sansome and have breakfast at the Poodle Dog. He arrived during the lull between the early and late breakfasters; midway through the meal he ordered sandwiches, boiled eggs, and beer to take Nat Green.

Green was waiting patiently at the warehouse when Foxx arrived. The cavernous building was still chilly from the night's wet fog; Green's eyes were watering and red from his all-night vigil and his nose was dripping, but he greeted Foxx cheerfully enough.

"I figured you'd be here about now." He saw the sack Foxx was carrying. "I hope that's breakfast. I'm starving."

Foxx passed the sack to Green. "Corned-beef sandwiches, hard-boiled eggs, and a couple of bottles of beer. Now, I know you're hungry, Nat, but don't start eating for a few minutes."

Green looked at Foxx with a puzzled frown but asked no questions.

"Did you have any trouble last night?" Foxx asked. "Did he say anything at all?"

"Not one damn peep out of him, Foxx. Not even when I made him take off his clothes." Green pointed to a heap of clothing on the floor beside the closet door.

Foxx looked around the long-abandoned building. It had been the center of the C&K's original San Francisco terminal before the depot and main offices were moved to the center of the city and the shops and roundhouse to the East Bay. High along the walls, grimed windows let a pallid suggestion of gray light trickle through. The effect at floor level was one of perpetual twilight. A lantern standing on the cracked bearing of a locomotive driver wheel still burned, its flame now almost invisible. Pigeonholes lined the walls, a checkerboard of dark squares. Dust lay an inch deep on the floor and on the odd bits and pieces of timbers, hunks of scrap metal, an oil-crusted bench, a broken-legged table, and other debris that had been left behind.

"Think you can find me a big nail or two in that mess of junk?" Foxx asked Green.

"Well, I found enough of a chair to sit on. I guess there's a few nails scattered around. You need it right now? I'm downright starved."

"Find me that nail, and you can sit down to breakfast without me bothering you."

Green kicked through the dust and scattered junk on the floor until he discovered a small pile of boxcar spikes. Wordlessly he held out a handful of the six-inch spikes to Foxx, who took one and picked up a short length of scrap iron that lay near the door of the closet.

"Now, Nat," Foxx said, "I'm going to let the busboy out. I want you to sit down and eat your breakfast pretty close by, where he can watch you. Leave one of the sandwiches and an egg, will you?"

"And that's all you want me to do?" Green sounded bewildered.

"That's all. Don't talk to me, don't talk to the bus-boy. Not even if he asks you something, or says something to you. As soon as you're through eating, get the hell out of here and go home. You're off duty until day after tomorrow. Maybe that'll make up for the time you put in last night."

Green shook his head but sat down on a length of railroad tie that was lying a few feet from the closet. He tore the sack open; it contained three sandwiches and four hard-boiled eggs. Spreading the sack flat on the tie, Green placed the food on the paper and un-wrapped one of the sandwiches.

Foxx kicked away the length of lumber that Green had used as a brace to keep the closet door shut. He pulled the door open, and the smell of excrement swept out of the opening. Foxx went into the closet and came out almost at once, leading the busboy by the chain that joined the handcuffs. The youth's naked body was smudged with dirt from the closet's interior. His legs were streaked with the marks of his night's voidings. The youth blinked and shut his eyes when the light hit them; even the twilight illumina-tion of the warehouse was blinding to someone who'd been confined in total darkness for ten or twelve hours.

Foxx did not speak. Without releasing his hold on the chain, he picked up the piece of scrap iron he'd laid close to the wall, shoved the boxcar spike through a link of the handcuff chain, and hoisted the prisoner's arms above his head. He forced the youth's back against the wall next to the closet door, keeping his arms high, and with the scrap iron for a hammer drove the spike into the wall. Foxx had moved so swiftly that the prisoner did not fully realize what was happening to him; he leaned against the wall, his arms sagging in the shackles that held them up, and continued to blink his eyes against the unaccustomed light.

Silently, Foxx stepped back and studied his captive. When seen naked the young man's physique confirmed Foxx's earlier guess that the busboy could not be past his earlier twenties. His bicep and calf muscles were well developed, but there was a soft roundness to his chest and stomach; the chest was lacking in the depth that maturity brings, and the stomach and abdomen were without the ridges of muscle common to active mature males. Although the busboy's face was still twitching as he blinked and squinted, Foxx was struck again by his conformity to the description the hobo had given of the dynamite setter. Nat Green, munching hungrily as he took alternate bites from a sandwich and an egg, watched Foxx and the prisoner but said nothing.

After several minutes the prisoner's eyes adjusted themselves to the light. He stared first at Foxx, then at Green, and turned back for a second look at Foxx. He opened his mouth as though he was about to speak but closed it at once.

Keeping his eyes fixed on the prisoner's face, Foxx sat down on the broken chair that Green had occupied. Except for the rustling noise made by the sandwich wrapper as Green pulled it away from the food to take a fresh bite, the silence in the warehouse was total.

A look of perplexed uncertainty crept over the prisoner's face as the minutes slowly ticked away. He began looking from Foxx to Green and back to Foxx again, his head swiveling slowly, his eyes worried, his brow furrowing as neither man spoke. Green continued to eat stolidly, paying no attention to the naked handcuffed youth. Foxx kept his eyes on the busboy. Each time the captive turned his head he found Foxx staring at him with an unblinking inscrutable expression.

In a short while the smell of the corned beef from Green's sandwiches began to waft through the area around the closet. More and more often now the prisoner's eyes turned to Nat Green, who was eating slowly, with obvious enjoyment. The youth jumped sharply when Green broke the shell of the third egg; in the dead silence of the warehouse the small snap of its cracking echoed like a pistol shot.

When the prisoner began to be affected by the smell of the food, Foxx knew that he had won the silent battle he'd set out to wage, the battle to force the youth to talk. Foxx did not enjoy using the Comanche trick of confining a prisoner in total darkness to disorient his sense of time, to make him think he'd been confined many hours, perhaps even days, and then letting him watch someone eating, to smell the food, and become aware of his own hunger and thirst.

Still, the staring trick was one of the most effective methods he'd ever found of forcing someone to talk without directly inflicting physical pain. There was something more torturing than pain in being stripped to the skin, in losing the continuity of night and day, of being unable to escape your own excrement, of being bound and helpless while undergoing the unwavering scrutiny of a silent foe. The prisoner's own fears were the instrument of his defeat. In the mind of the helpless captive, images of degrading and painful torture began to form, and ultimately the unending stare of his captor rasped on frayed nerves and brought on the collapse of even the strongest will.

Foxx had never been as good at the eye torture as had the Comanches who'd taught it to him. He had never been able to match their patience. During his youth as a member of the Comanche tribe by forced adoption, the young Comanches with whom he was being taught the eye torment by the older warriors could always outlast him in keeping their gaze fixed and their features frozen. And Foxx had seen old Comanche warriors stare at a captured enemy, a Pawnee or Cheyenne or Arapahoe, for two full days and nights without stirring or shifting their eyes.

On the few previous occasions when Foxx had used the eye torture against other white men, he'd learned to gauge the crumbling of resistance by their reaction to the smell of food being cooked or eaten in front of them. He watched the prisoner now for further signs, and smiled inwardly when the youth's jaws started working unconsciously as he watched Nat Green chewing, and his Adam's apple began bobbing as he swallowed the juices that were flooding his mouth.

Green kept biting pieces off the sandwich and chewing them slowly. The prisoner's reflex imitation of the detective's motions continued until Green had finished the sandwich and egg and had drained his beer bottle and tossed it empty to the floor. Even though the youth had been watching Green, he jumped involuntarily when the bottle crashed on the cinder-covered ground.

Foxx used the moments while the busboy's attention was riveted on Green to relax his stiffening neck and shoulder muscles by moving his head. He saw Green turning to look at him, and nodded almost imperceptibly. Green did not acknowledge the signal, but stood up and started walking leisurely to the door. The prisoner's eyes followed Green's every step until he'd closed the warehouse door behind him.

When the youth looked at Foxx again, he found himself facing the same unwavering stare and graven face that had haunted him since he'd been taken from the closet. His body had slumped a bit as the strain of holding his arms up to keep the steel handcuffs from cutting into his wrists became an unbearable drain on his already-lowered resources. He brought himself erect now and tried to outstare Foxx.

Foxx acted as though the prisoner had neither moved nor changed the nature of his expression, and after a few moments the youth gave up the effort. Abruptly he turned his eyes away from Foxx and began to gaze around the huge empty building. Like a magnet, though, Foxx again drew his attention. The youth faced Foxx again and began returning his stare. The second effort lasted only half as long as the first. Foxx gave an inward sigh of relief, for the captive's reaction told him that the long period of motionless impassive staring was almost at an end.

Foxx's judgment proved correct. The prisoner did not try to outstare him again. After a few minutes he looked back at Foxx, but this time he avoided locking eyes. He opened his mouth and closed it, squeezed his eyes shut for a moment, and when he opened them again his mouth began to gush words.

"Listen, mister," he began, "I've held out as long as I can. You and that other fellow haven't got no right to keep a man locked up the way you got me, bare-ass naked in the dark, and nothing to eat or drink for two days or more. Now, tell me what you're after. I didn't really hurt nobody, remember. I guess you can put me up in front of a judge, but all he'll give me is a little time in jail. Ain't that right?" He waited for Foxx to reply, but Foxx remained silent. The youth started again.

"Look here, I bet you're figuring to try some kind of deviltry on me! Maybe cut off my fingers one at a time or slit my nose like a Paiute would or build a fire on my belly or something like that. But you don't need to do anything else! Look here, I'm spittin' cotton and about to starve to death. You give me that sandwich over there, and I'll tell the judge what I done without making you no more trouble. Go on, tell me what you want me to say! I'll do whatever you want!"

When Foxx neither replied nor shifted his gaze, the youth stared wildly at him for a few seconds before he spoke again. This time he raised his voice to a shout. "Don't you hear me? Damn it, I heard you talk the other night, I know you ain't deaf! Say something, damn it!"

Foxx continued to stare and still did not speak. After a short silence, a puzzled frown formed on the prisoner's face. He tried again. "Listen to me, now. I know you ain't a regular policeman. You work for the railroad, ain't that right?" He paused expectantly, and when he saw that Foxx was not going to reply, went on. "Oh, you work for the damn railroad, all right. I heard enough the other night to find that out. So maybe you can't take me to jail? Maybe you got to settle up private for me taking a shot at you and that potbellied old bastard. Well, hell, I guess I know better'n to try anything like that again. Look, mister, you let me go this time, and I swear I won't bother nobody from the railroad again. Ain't that a fair and square proposition?"

Foxx maintained his silent staring. The youth said desperately, "Well, damn it! What in hell else are you after? You want to know who I am? Is that right? All right, I'll tell you. My name's Ed—Ed Jones, that is. And when you started running after me there at that party the other night, I got scared. Now, I'll tell you the gospel truth. I was just out to steal whatever I could pick up outa that place. I run outa money and had to get back home, to—to over in Utah. I tried to hop a freight, but the damned brakeman throwed me off. So I got mad at the railroad, that's why I picked out that railroad shindy to rob. Now you know everything I can tell you. Why don't you just call it quits and turn me loose?"

While his prisoner had been talking, Foxx had

been trying to sift the truth from the lies he knew he was hearing. His effort at eye torture had been only half successful. He'd forced the captive to talk, but not to tell the truth. He doubted that anything further he did would have any better chance of succeeding.

While he was still trying to work out an alternative plan, the captive started talking again. The youth's mood had changed now from desperation to defiance. His lips were thin, his eyes angry. He said, "All right, damn you! Go ahead! Cut me up or kill me or do whatever you been setting there figuring to do! I got nothing else to tell you!"

Foxx had heard enough. He stood up, still silent, and walked over to the prisoner. The self-named Ed Jones flinched as Foxx approached, but quickly straightened up and stared at Foxx challengingly. Foxx reached up to the handcuffs and worked the boxcar spike up and down until it was loose enough to be pulled from the wall. He took the youth's arm, slick now with the sweat of fear, and shoved him back into the closet. Slamming the door, Foxx replaced the brace that Green had used to wedge the door closed.

In the stillness of the warehouse he heard clearly the animallike howls that the prisoner was uttering. The last thing Foxx heard as he left the warehouse was the clatter of the youth's handcuffed wrists beating on the closet door.

CHAPTER 7

Foxx glanced at the clear blue sky as he left the warehouse and was surprised to see that the sun was not yet noon high. He felt as though he'd been there for a full day. The eye torture had its effect on both the victim and the one employing it; it dislocated the time sense of both. He lighted a stogie, the first he'd had since he began trying to wear down the prisoner's resistance. Lighting a cigar would have destroyed the impact of the eye torture.

Walking hurriedly, Foxx headed for the police call box he remembered as being near the warehouse. By arrangement with the San Francisco Police Department, members of private police forces employed by all the railroads and banks carried keys to these boxes. They were also familiar with the simple police codes used by officers walking their beats. Adapted from the Morse telegraph, the signal buttons in the boxes were used by patrolmen on their beats to transmit to the closest precinct station a number of simple messages. There were codes indicating that the officer had reached the box in the course of making his rounds, that a paddy wagon was needed, that a fire had broken out, that a riot was in progress, or that the officer needed help.

Opening the box, Foxx pressed the signal button three times. In the nearest precinct station a buzzer sounded and a marker dropped to show the location of the box where the call originated. Foxx closed the box and settled back to wait.

His wait was not a long one. Within ten minutes a paddy wagon rumbled up, two uniformed policemen on its seat. The one holding the reins pulled up the horses in front of the box, and the officers stepped down.

"Where's Muldoon?" one of them asked. "And what kind of trouble is he in?"

"Muldoon would be the beat officer?" Foxx asked. He took out his C&K badge and showed it to the other two. "Foxx is my name. Chief of detectives for the C&K."

"Oh, sure, I've heard about you," the other officer said. He looked around the deserted street. "Well, what kind of trouble have you got here? You railroad cops usually like to handle your own cases without us coming into it unless it's something pretty serious."

"This one isn't that bad," Foxx told him. "What I really need is a favor from you."

"Like what?"

"I've got a man shut up in that old C&K storehouse down the street. I guess you know the one I mean?" When the policeman nodded, Foxx went on. "He's a stubborn young bastard. I got him started talking, but most of what he told me was lies. What I—"

"Wait a minute," the second policeman interrupted. "What'd this fellow do? If it's some bum you want us to roust—"

Foxx did the interrupting this time. "He's not. He tried to shoot Caleb Petersen last night. Took a shot at me, too, but that's not important. Now, I've got a damn good hunch that this man's also connected with another one who put a couple of sticks of dynamite on our tracks over in Solano County night before last."

One of the policemen whistled. "That's serious enough, I guess. What'd you call us for, though?"

"I want you to take this fellow to your precinct holdover and keep him there until late this evening. Don't book him. Just lock him up in your holdover and let him go about six o'clock."

"That's a funny thing to ask us to do," one of the officers said, with a frown. "You mind saying why?"

"No. It's not this man I'm after; I want the one who put that dynamite on our tracks. You men know enough about bombers to know they don't give up trying. I'm counting on the one in the storehouse to lead me to him. I think the man I'm looking for is his brother or cousin, or some kind of close relative."

"Hell, turn the one you've got over to our boys downtown," the policeman suggested. "After they've had him down in the basement an hour or two, he'll tell you anything you want to know."

Foxx shook his head. "I wish it was that easy. I've got a basement of my own, but from what I've seen of this fellow, it'd be a waste of time using it. He's young, but he's tough. And he's a pretty good liar, to boot." He fished a pair of twenty-dollar gold pieces out of his pocket. "I'd appreciate it if you'd lend me a hand on this." He handed each man one of the double eagles. "Here's a little something for your Police Benevolent Association fund, just a little thank-you from the C&K." Foxx knew quite well the PBA treasury would never see a penny of the money. Twenty dollars was almost a half-month's pay for one of San Francisco's uniformed policemen.

"Well, I don't see why we can't oblige you, Foxx," one of the officers said.

"Sure," his companion chimed in. "It's not a hell of a big favor. Let's be sure we know what to do, now. Just keep the fellow in the holdover at the precinct house and turn him loose about six o'clock."

"That's right," Foxx replied. "I'll be there to start tailing him." He added, "Oh, don't be surprised when you see the man. You'll have to use your handcuff key to let him get his arms free so he can put his clothes on. And snap the padlock on the outside door of the storehouse when you leave. Then I won't have to go back there."

Foxx did not leave the neighborhood, though, until he'd seen the policemen come out of the warehouse with the busboy and put him in the paddy wagon. Then he walked over to Portilla and caught the trolleycar that took him to Market Street, where he could find a cab.

"Let him go!" Jim Flaherty's jaw dropped as he gazed across his desk at Foxx. "You're out of your mind, Foxx!"

"You might be right, Jim. But it's the easiest and fastest way I can see to get hold of the one who set that dynamite."

"Suppose he gives you the slip?"

"He won't. From what he told me without knowing it, I've got a pretty good idea where he'll head, anyhow."

"Where?"

"I'd say along the south part of Idaho Territory, close to where they busted off Nevada when it was made a state. Or he might've come from Nevada, up where our trackage runs north into that corner of Idaho Territory."

"What's that got to do with it?"

"Stands to reason, as long as we're pretty sure that dynamite was set to get back at us for something he figures the C&K did to him or his folks. He's sure to've come from someplace along our trackage."

"But why Idaho or Nevada?" Flaherty frowned.

"Because he told me he lived in Utah Territory."

"Then—"

"He was lying. But I got a look at his hands. They're rancher's hands, Jim. So, chances are he's off a ranch along that stretch of mainline between the Parapets and the Utah line. It's not going to be any trick to tail him, not in that part of the country. There's not all that many places where there's water enough for ranching, and not many more where there's even enough for people. What few ranches stand close to our line along there are mostly run by families, which makes it even a more likely place for him to be going to."

"I guess you've already checked up on accident and claim reports to see if there's any problems with ranchers there?"

"I haven't. But I set Pat Kelly to working on that side of it. Godamighty, Jim! You have any idea how many claims we've had just from that little stretch? Pat's got a stack of papers two feet high to plow through."

"You ever think of staying to help him look, instead of kiting off on what might be a wild-goose chase?" Flaherty asked.

"Oh, sure. I thought about it, just like I thought about holding that busboy here until somebody comes looking for him. But that'd take too long. We sure don't want to give the one that's partial to dynamite time to try again. He might make a go of it next time."

Flaherty pursed his lips thoughtfully. "I guess you've got a good point there, Foxx. But this fellow you're going to tail out tonight, did you ever stop to think he could hop a Central Pacific drag out of the East Bay as easy as he could one of ours? Or that there might be somebody waiting for him, and they'd take off on horseback?"

"If I was damn fool enough not to think about

things like that, you wouldn't be hiring me. No, Jim. I'm betting my man's going to hop Number Nine about the time it leaves the Oakland yards tonight at eight. And I'm betting he won't get off it short of someplace in that corner where the three territories join."

"What if he doesn't?"

"Then I'll find him again, damn it! If I have to look on every ranch between here and the Mississippi River!"

Flaherty grinned. "You'd do that, too, if you had to, I guess. Oh, hell, Foxx, we both know you're going ahead the way you think is best. Why am I wasting time arguing with you?"

It was Foxx's turn to grin now. It was a short grin, and when it faded he said very soberly, "I'll guarantee you this, Jim. If he does give me the slip, it won't be for very long."

All the possibilities Flaherty had brought up during their talk had already occurred to Foxx. He'd also planned his precautions. Before leaving the C&K building he visited the chief dispatcher's office and sent messages over the C&K's telegraph wire to stationmasters along the line to the east. They were, he instructed them, to tell their crews not to comb Number Nine for hoboes when it stopped at their stations. He sent a similar message to Anderson, across the bay. Neither the yard bulls nor the brakemen were to roust hoboes out of the yards or off the night freight when it pulled out.

Having protected his flanks as best he could, Foxx visited the paymaster's office and drew expense money for his trip. He got the money in twenty- and fifty-dollar gold pieces, knowing how reluctant ranchers and merchants in isolated areas were to accept greenbacks. As Foxx left the offices, he saw by the big clock in the foyer that he still had almost three hours to wait before going to the South San Francisco police precinct station to pick up the trail of his man. He thought briefly of stepping into a cab and spending an hour or so with Vida Martin, but the temptation passed quickly. Instead, he went back to his hotel suite. He had his traveling kit to check, and if any of Jim Flaherty's gloomy possibilities occurred, Foxx knew he might be on the road for quite a while.

Foxx preferred to travel light. Given his choice, he'd have carried his needs in two or three small pouches, as the Comanches had taught him to do. Since this was impractical in a civilization that judged traveling strangers by their clothing and their luggage, he bowed to convention; not to have done so would have caused strangers to notice him, and this was not always desirable. However, unless he knew that a case was apt to involve extremes of time and distance and prolonged stays in cities, he seldom carried more than one small valise.

This valise had been made for Foxx as a favor by Carstairs, his favorite San Francisco bootmaker. The small leather case was always kept locked. It was exactly large enough to hold a pair of boots placed toes-up at opposite ends. In the toe of one boot was Foxx's spare razor and a gutta-percha case containing a round of shaving soap. His shaving brush and a comb wrapped in handkerchiefs went in the toe of the other boot.

Because most of Foxx's cases kept him outdoors in all kinds of weather, the boots that he usually kept in the valise were a pair cobbled from thick-split and virtually waterproof walrus-hide uppers and buffalo-hide soles. Foxx was sure they would keep his feet dry even in the wettest weather.

Inside the leg of one boot, tightly rolled, was a linen singlet, a pair of longjohns knitted from the finest merino wool, and a pair each of light cotton and

heavy wool socks. The other bootleg held a denim
shirt and a heavier shirt of Swaldale woolen cloth. A
pair of Levi denim miner's jeans was folded to fit in
the curving upper part of the valise. Nestled in the
folds of the jeans was a revolver, whichever one he
chose not to carry on his person. A box of cartridges
for each of the guns and a dozen strips of venison
jerky wrapped in oiled paper completed his field outfit.

To complete his packing for the present trip, Foxx
needed only to decide which gun he'd wear. He chose
the forty-four Smith and Wesson; in the country
where he was confident his trip would end, range and
stopping power were more important than weight
and bulk. He took his Colt House revolver from the
sewed-in pocket holster of the coat he had on and
tucked it into the valise. There was no need for Foxx
to check either weapon; he kept his guns in perfect
condition at all times.

There were only one or two minor matters left.
Foxx glanced through the bedroom door at the big
Railroad Regulator hanging on the wall of his suite's
sitting room to see how much time remained before
he had to begin what would certainly be a long and
almost sleepless night. Foxx set his mental alarm to
wake him in an hour, pulled off his boots, and
stretched out on the bed.

Promptly at four thirty, when the hour he'd allot-
ted himself was up, Foxx snapped awake. There was
no period of yawning drowsiness between sleeping
and waking. When his eyes opened, Foxx was alert
and functioning fully. He swung his legs over the side
of the bed and stood up in the same swift movement,
then padded to the bathroom on sock-clad feet. When
he returned to the bedroom, he put the decorated
boots he'd worn earlier in the closet and selected a
pair of cordovan saddle-leather boots with cavalry
heels.

His boots on, Foxx removed his belt and laid it flat on the dresser. He dug the rolls of coins that he'd drawn from the C&K paymaster from his coat pocket and peeled open the thin overlapping layers of sheepskin with which the belt was lined; after he'd filled the U-shaped pouches in the inner fold, he still had more than two hundred dollars in coins. He put these into his pocket after replacing the belt.

Strapping on his holstered Smith and Wesson American, Foxx shrugged into coat and vest, lifted the wide-brimmed brown Borsalino hat he preferred to wear in the field, and picked up his valise. He dropped a silver dollar on the small table by the sitting-room door, a signal to the chambermaid that he'd be out of town and that the job of winding the Railroad Regulator once a week would fall to her. The Regulator was just striking five when Foxx closed the door of the suite and started down the stairs.

"Go on past the police station to the middle of the block and turn around to head toward town," Foxx told the driver of the hack that had brought him from the Cosmopolitan Hotel. "Pull up as soon as you've turned your rig. We'll sit for a while."

With a squeal of an ungreased transom pin and a creaking of leather reins, the hackman turned the carriage and pulled the horse to a halt on the opposite side of the street. Foxx leaned back in a corner of the closed cab, where he could watch the door of the precinct house through the hack's open side window. He dug one of the twisted black cigars off the fresh bundle he'd slipped into his coat pocket and lighted it. The pungent smoke from the overripened maduro soon filled the carriage.

Foxx smoked the cigar down to a stub and was reaching for another when the door of the precinct station opened and the busboy came out. He stood in front of the station house a minute, looking both ways along the street. Foxx leaned back further in the shadowed interior of the hack when the youth's eyes stopped on the carriage, but apparently he thought it normal for a hack to be waiting in front of a house a good distance from where he was standing. He looked at the carriage for a moment without any obvious curiosity, and then his gaze traveled on along the street. In a moment he began walking purposefully, and Foxx guessed that he'd gotten directions from one of the policemen before leaving the precinct station.

Foxx waited until the busboy had gotten well ahead of the hack before telling the driver, "Go ahead, now, but keep a rein on your nag. I want you to keep me in sight of that fellow walking along up there, but I don't want you to get too close to him."

"You're the boss," the hackman said, picking up the reins. He slapped them lightly on the horse's rump, and the animal began moving at a slow clopping walk.

At that hour and in that part of town, the streets were almost clear of traffic. The hackman kept the carriage well behind the walking busboy, even after he turned into Third Street and started north. Foxx relaxed. He was more positive than ever that the youth had asked for directions to the ferry slip.

As the street curved, following the contours of the waterfront, and they drew closer to downtown, traffic on both street and sidewalk thickened. Foxx leaned forward and craned his neck out of the window, but now and again he lost sight of his quarry for several moments at a time. When they neared Market Street, he had still more trouble keeping the youth in sight.

"Wait until that fellow I'm following turns onto Market," he instructed the cabman. "As soon as he's around the corner, pull ahead of him. Stop short of the corner until we get to Fremont. Then let him get ahead of us again and keep behind him."

On the long blocks that characterized Market Street above First, Foxx knew that the busboy would have no side streets to take. He felt perfectly safe in letting the youth out of sight; there was little doubt now as to his destination.

Leapfrogging, alternately ahead of and behind the busboy, Foxx leaning back in the carriage each time they passed him or he passed the cab, Foxx kept sight of the walking youth without difficulty.

Once across Fremont, the number of pedestrians thinned out. When the busboy reached the Embarcadero and made straight for the ferry slip, Foxx was sure of what the youth's next move would be. He ordered the cabbie to speed up and got to the slip well in advance of the busboy. High on the upper deck of the ferryboat that was loading, Foxx watched the youth come aboard. Then he picked up his valise, retired to the upper deck saloon, and at a table in the darkest corner, with a stein of steam beer and a plate of tiny bay shrimp in front of him, he relaxed while the paddlewheeler churned across to the Oakland side.

Like every railroader in northern California, Foxx knew the location of the permanent hobo jungles. In Oakland the bindlestiffs favored a spot on the estuary midway between the C&K and the Southern Pacific yards. There was a smaller jungle on the other side of the narrow tongue of tidewater where the Central Pacific yards and shops were located, but so far Foxx had seen little reason to change his mind about the busboy's immediate and ultimate destinations.

He let the youth take the lead in the deepening dusk and dogged behind him until the half-dozen fires of the main jungle gleamed just ahead. Then Foxx fell back. He was able now to identify the youth by his silhouetted figure alone as the busboy moved between the fires, stopping briefly at two before settling down at the third. Foxx took out his repeater watch, opened the case, and pressed the chime lever. The tiny delicate tinkling told him that Number Nine was due to pull out of the yards in a quarter of an hour. He circled the edge of the jungle until he crossed the path beaten by the Weary Willies from their gathering place to the point where the C&K rails left the yard boundaries. He stopped there, to wait again.

Beyond the fires of the jungle he could see the glow of the Southern Pacific's yards and shops. Behind him the C&K's yard lights made a puddle of brightness in the evening sky. There was a constant undertone of noise where Foxx stood: the sharp yelp of yard dinkies, an occasional crash and clash of couplings as a boxcar was shunted to join a forming string, the lighter echoes of brakemen's voices shouting, and always the metallic humming of machine shop and roundhouse sounds.

Soon the hoboes began to move. Some of them drifted toward the SP yards and vanished in the darkness, but the majority headed for the C&K tracks. Foxx kept his eyes on the silhouette of the busboy and saw him join the uneven line of boes moving toward the C&K yard limits. As the first of the hoboes approached, Foxx stepped away from the path, even though there was little chance he'd be recognized, or even noticed, for night had arrived while he was waiting. He moved parallel with the center of the group until the leaders stopped a score of yards beyond the point where the silver streaks of C&K rails showed in the darkness, then slowly worked his way past those first in line and turned back to wach.

There was, Foxx knew, an unofficial and unspoken agreement between the hoboes and the brakemen and yard police. As long as the knights of the road stayed

fifty feet or more from the yard's boundaries, they
would be free from rousting. However, any bo entering the yards to hop a freight while it was creeping
even more slowly than it moved just after passing the
"Yard Limits" sign beside the tracks could expect a
few lusty kicks at best and a billy-clubbing at worst if
he was caught.

There were perhaps twenty men in the straggling
line of hoboes that now began to form beside the
tracks. They spaced themselves the rough equivalent
of a boxcar's length apart, partners together, most of
them alone. Hoboes learned as quickly as railroaders
that a moving car should always be boarded at its
front end. There, a missed jump or slipped grip
meant that the man would be thrown back against
the side of the boxcar and fall to the roadbed. A bad
grab at a car's back end usually caused the man to be
swung back into the space between two cars and a
mangling or sudden death under the next car's
wheels.

From the yards a whistle sounded, closer than most,
and in a moment the headlight of Number Nine
lighted up the track. The hoboes let the first half-
dozen boxcars in the string pass by, then moved up to
the roadbed and began swinging aboard. Foxx waited
until the last of them was on the train and ran along
beside the end cars until he could hop aboard. He
made a one-hand grab for the bar grip, holding his
valise in his other hand. Then, as Number Nine gained
speed, he climbed the ladder between cars and walked
the topboards back until he reached the caboose.

Ahead of him, Foxx knew, the man he was trailing
was safely aboard. He would need no watching until
the freight slowed at the Carquinez Straits to be
trundled aboard the railroad ferry.

Satisfied, Foxx fished one of his twisted stogies out
of his vest pocket and cupped his hands around the
match while he lighted it. Then he leaned back

against the end of the caboose, not wanting to go inside yet, enjoying the pungent smoke of the stogie and the night wind streaming across his face as the train picked up speed.

CHAPTER 8

Foxx finished his cigar and stubbed the butt out on the brake handle before tossing it away. The train had reached its maximum speed for the stretch through the Berkeley hills and was swaying as it took the curves. Foxx picked up his valise and went into the caboose. There was only one man in the car. He was putting kindling in the potbellied stove that stood in the center of the bay. Foxx introduced himself.

"Sure," the man said. "I've heard about you, but this is the first time you've rode a drag I was crewing. I'm Emil Sterner, the conductor.

"Sterner." Foxx nodded, keeping the surprise out of his voice. On western railroads, the operating crewmen were predominantly Irish, while men of German and Scottish origin gravitated to the shops and roundhouses. Foxx glanced around the caboose and asked, "Where's the rest of the crew?"

"Oh, we'll have the crummy to ourselves until we cross the straits," Sterner told him. "I've got the tailend spot, of course, so I don't have much to do right now. But the brakemen have to dog the wheels when we board the ferry and knock the dogs loose when we get off, so they stay with the cars until we start rolling on the Solano side."

"I see. What about the boes, Sterner? Do you let them stay on while the string's crossing?"

"Sometimes we do, sometimes we don't. If there's just a few, we usually let 'em stay on. If there's a big bunch, more'n we can handle if there's trouble, we roust 'em. They'll stay on tonight, though. We got orders to let 'em alone."

"I know. I had that put in the train orders."

"I guess it's not any of my business, but my whole crew's been wondering about that."

"There's no secret about it. I had an idea that a man I'm trailing would hop Number Nine along with the bindlestiffs tonight, and I didn't want him to get tossed off."

"Did he get on, then?" the conductor asked.

"Yes. And I want him to be let alone until he's ready to get off. I'd turn out with you and walk the drag, but he'll recognize me if he sees me, and start running. What I'd like for you to do is pass the word up the string that none of the bindlestiffs is to be let off at the ferry."

"I don't think you need to worry about that, Mr. Foxx. The boes generally work along the drag as soon as they hop on and find an empty they can hole up in. We know where they are, of course, even if they pull the car doors closed, but the only time we worry much about 'em is in winter, when they might start a fire in the car to keep warm."

"Well, it's too early for it to get that cold," Foxx said. He knew the habits of the hoboes as well as the conductor did. "Now, so you'll know this fellow, he's young, medium tall, got a straight nose, dark hair. Needs a shave, but I guess most of the boes do, too. He hasn't got on a coat, and his shirt's fairly clean. Dark pants, and his shoes are in better shape than most of the boes."

"I'll get the word moving up front, then." Sterner hesitated a moment, then asked, "Can you tell me why you're set on nabbing this man, Mr. Foxx?"

"I'm counting on him to lead me to the fellow who tried to dynamite our line over in Solano County a few nights ago."

Sterner whistled. "I heard about that. Well, you don't have to worry, Mr. Foxx. When my men know why you're after him, I'll just about guarantee we'll keep him aboard. You have any idea where he's heading for?"

"It'll be east of the Sierra, I'm pretty sure. My guess is anywhere from halfway across Nevada to just over the Utah line. But it could be anyplace between the Parapets and Utah."

Sterner was drawing on his gloves. He said, "We'll just keep all the boes on board until we're out of the mountains, then, if that's all right with you. The boys know which empties the Willies are in; they usually divide up between two or three cars. We'll just latch the doors and hatches when we break the string to get on the ferry."

"Good," Foxx agreed. "After we get through the mountains, you can unbutton the cars at the first water stop. And from there on, I'll be up in the cupola watching the cars at every stop. I want to be sure to spot him when he leaves."

Foxx stretched out on one of the caboose bunks after the conductor left and let the rhythmic clicking of the wheels over the rail joints lull him to sleep. He woke when the brakes began grinding to slow the train for the ferry stop and climbed into the cupola. If, as Flaherty had suggested, the busboy and the dynamite setter had arranged to meet, the ferry slip on one side or other of the Carquinez crossing might be a logical spot for them to have chosen.

Climbing into the cupola, Foxx lighted a stogie and settled back to watch. On top of the boxcars the brakemen were stationing themselves to be ready to uncouple the cars at the spots where the freight would be broken down into lengths short enough to be accommodated on the ferryboat's parallel sets of rails. A brakeman disappeared between two cars, and Foxx heard the distant clunk of a link and pin coupling being opened. The first section of cars moved creepingly ahead and came to a halt on the broad deck of the ferry.

Now the ferry's dinky engine took over. It steamed up from its siding and stopped just short of touching the caboose. Foxx saw Sterner in the glow of the conductor's signal lantern, waving the dinky ahead. The freight cars moved slowly forward as the dinky pushed them; the first cars swerved into the siding and were pushed onto the boat. The maneuver was repeated three times before the entire train was aboard the ferry, then the screw-propelled ferryboat plowed across the treacherous currents of Carquinez Strait to the opposite shore, where the freight's engineer took over and reassembled the train.

Then they were on the main line again, out of the pool of light that bathed the ferry slip, steaming at speed across the flat, featureless delta country. Foxx could not see the land in the darkness, but he'd been over the route so many times that he knew the trackage by heart. The three brakemen straggled into the caboose, hung up their caps and lanterns, and began wiping their hands on bundles of fluffy waste. Foxx waited until Sterner came in, and then climbed down from the cupola.

"We've got three cars of hoboes buttoned up," Sterner reported. "None of 'em tried to get off, so I guess your man's still aboard."

"Good," Foxx said. "Now, just be sure you don't cut any of the cars they're in when you switch at Sacramento."

"There's nothing on the manifest to be cut there

tonight," the conductor replied. "We've got a few cars to pick up, and a few that're consigned there to cut out, but that's all. Your man ought to be safe until we unlock the empties at the division yards in Carlin."

"Looks like I don't have much to worry about for a while, then," Foxx said. "Thanks, Sterner. Now, I don't want to get in your way. I'll just sit back in a corner of the bay, and you men go on about your business."

"There's not much business between stops on a freight, Mr. Foxx," Sterner smiled. "We usually deal a few hands of cards between stops. Double pedro," he added hastily. "Not poker or anything like that. I won't let anybody break Rule 36 while I'm in charge. But what I started to say was, if you'd care to sit in with us, you'll sure be welcome."

"I appreciate the invitation, but I think I'll pass this time," Foxx answered. "I'm not much of a hand at pedro."

Foxx fired up a stogie and settled back in the bay to watch the pedro game. It lasted until the engineer whistled for the Sacramento River bridge crossing. The whistle broke up the game; the players dropped their cards and hurried to their positions, each man responsible for a specific number of cars in an assigned section of the train. Sterner went out to the back platform, carrying his signal lantern. Foxx climbed the ladder to the cupola and watched while the cars to be cut were shunted onto sidings and several new ones added to the string. The job was done quickly, and within a half hour Number Nine was on its way again, steaming northeast toward the Sierra foothills.

Looking down from the cupola into the bay, Foxx saw Sterner return to the caboose, followed in a short while by the brakemen. The four resumed their interrupted game of double pedro. Foxx climbed down and watched the game for a few minutes, then decided that storing up a bit of sleep against the uncertainties of the immediate future was a better idea. He moved to one of the bunks in the back of the caboose, took off his gunbelt and coat, and stretched out. Sleep was slow in coming. The swaying of the caboose as Number Nine entered the first of many sinuous stretches of track that lay ahead set him to thinking about the C&K's often rocky and always risky earlier days.

Caleb Petersen had come late to the western railroad scene. Stanford, Hopkins, Huntington, and Crocker had already bought the failing Southern Pacific and were building south to Los Angeles. They'd stolen Caleb's plan to push trackage south and then extend the road's main line eastward.

He'd intended to follow the old Whipple survey, a route which skirted the toes of the Sierras and Rockies, crossed what was still called the Great American Desert, and then cut through the Texas panhandle and Indian Territory to the banks of the Arkansas River at Fort Smith. Caleb had not planned to follow Whipple's route that far; his idea had been to angle northeast from Texas into Kansas City, tapping the new cattle ranges and the fertile wheatlands of those areas for freight.

Caleb had found the Big Four ahead of him. Quietly, they had been buying rights of way south—using the vast reservoir of cash siphoned out of the Central Pacific's government subsidies by their Credit & Finance subsidiary, Caleb always swore—through California's Central Valley and along the state's coastline as well. Caleb changed his plans quickly. He began pushing rails northeast from Sacramento through a series of valleys that sliced in a zigzag across the Sierra Nevada and on to Idaho and the upper edge of Utah.

From there C&K survey teams found passes not already preempted by the Union Pacific that took C&K

iron over the Rockies south of the Great Divide Basin of Wyoming, and then still other passes through the Wind River and Sweetwater ranges of the eastern Rockies. The road finally lived up to its name when it cut southeast, cut across the tips of Colorado and Nebraska and entered Kansas.

By the time Foxx had followed the C&K through the Wind River and Sweetwater ranges, he was yawning. When his thinking finally got the rails to Kansas City, sleep caught up with him.

A change in the tempo of the caboose's rattling and swaying brought Foxx awake. The pedro game had broken up, and snores of several different degrees of intensity and tone filled the caboose. Foxx rolled out of the bunk and stretched. The lantern hanging from a chain between the sides of the bay was dimmed by the gray light that was stealing through the windows. Before Foxx had finished stretching, Sterner came through the caboose's forward door. Foxx leaned forward to peer out the window.

"We're just starting downgrade to the water tower at the Parapets, I'd say," he told Sterner. "And that means I must've slept right on through the tower stop at the Yuba."

"You know the road pretty well, Mr. Foxx. You've called the spot to a tee. I just came in to rouse the men to get up on top for the downgrade."

There was no need for Sterner to rouse the brakemen; they'd been awakened by the voices of Foxx and the conductor or by the change in the caboose's vibrations. They were already on their feet, pulling caps over sleep-tousled heads or donning gloves. They pushed past Foxx and Sterner with cursory nods or grunts and went out to their stations.

Foxx asked, "Have you unlatched the hoboes' cars yet?"

"No. I intend to at the tower stop, though. Unless you've changed your mind?"

"No. It's daylight now. I'll be able to see both sides of the train when I get back up in the cupola. Go ahead and open the cars when we stop."

"You know, I think it might be a good idea if I strapped on my pistol belt," Sterner said thoughtfully. "Those men have been locked in for more than eight hours, and there's usually a few ugly customers among 'em."

"You mean they might be mad at your men because the cars were locked?" Foxx frowned. "Damn it, they're on this train on sufferance. They've got no right to be riding, if push comes to shove."

Sterner smiled a bit grimly. "You'll never convince the boes of that, Mr. Foxx. They've got their own rules and laws, and one of them seems to be that we owe them free transportation."

"I know they've got their own rules, just like the roads do, but I'd never heard that they think we owe them anything."

"Oh, I don't suppose most of them do. They're generally a pretty peaceful lot, just men like the rest of us, only down on their luck. There's a few bad apples in the barrel, though, and they try to make trouble."

"If you're expecting trouble—" Foxx began, but Sterner held up his hand.

"No, Mr. Foxx. I'm not expecting anything to happen. I just like to be ready if something does. I guess you've heard that a bunch of bindlestiffs beat up a U.P. yardman a couple of weeks ago, in Ogallala?"

"I hadn't heard about that. Damn it, you men on the operating crews get news faster than I do."

"I just heard about it myself," Sterner said. "But I'll bet every hobo in those cars up the drag has. So I'll just be ready and wear my pistol belt."

"Good idea," Foxx agreed. "I'll keep my eyes peeled. I'm going to be up in the cupola. The man I'm trailing might get off; if he does, I want to see him."

Looking out of the window of the cupola, chewing on a strip of jerky from his valise, Foxx could scan the entire length of the train. The cupola rose like a turret above the tops of the cars, and its four windows also showed the terrain on both sides of the track and to the rear. The brakemen were running from car to car, jumping the yard-wide gap between each car, grabbing at brake wheels and tightening them down to keep the couplings tight and prevent the cars from pushing the engine out of control.

At the foot of the long grade they were descending, the alkali flats of the northern Nevada desertland looked like snow fields in the gray predawn light. Behind the train the rising sun was touching the gray granite tips of the Sierra peaks and flushing them to a delicate pink. On the flanks of the mountains bordering the downslope the pine forest still appeared black and mysterious, the tracks a sinuous snakelike ribbon cutting through them.

Ahead, a spurt of steam shot from the locomotive's whistle, and seconds later the toot reached Foxx's ears. Now the brakemen went back to work, slacking up the brakes they'd set in such a frenzied rush. The engine was already on the flats, and soon the entire train was on the level ground. In the near distance the triple spires of the Parapets rose like the towers of a medieval fortress from the level desert.

Their work done for the moment, the brakemen were now sitting down on the tops of the boxcars that marked one end of their assigned sections. The Parapets loomed larger and larger ahead, and soon the whistle sounded once more. The brakemen stood up, ready to grab the big cast-iron brake wheels when the freight came to a stop. The rattling of coupling pins began again as the engineer slowed speed. Then the noise ended and the desert silence took over. The brakeman at the head of the string gave his brake wheel a final twist and dropped out of sight between the boxcar and engine. In a moment, the engine and tender moved on alone, away from the train, to the wooden-stave water tower that was almost hidden between the Parapets.

With the cars motionless, the other brakemen also clambered to the ground. They walked along their sections, checking the cars' journal boxes for signs of overheating and inspecting the wheels for damage to their flanges. As they passed the boxcars where the hoboes had been confined, the brakemen removed the toggles that had secured the sliding doors. On hearing the clinking of the toggles being pulled, the hoboes slid the car doors open, dropping to the ground. Foxx counted nine of them. The brakeman who'd unlatched the door was at the end of the next car in the string, bending down to check the wheels and journals. The little group of hoboes made for him as one man.

Foxx was too far away to hear what was being said, but it was obvious that angry words were being exchanged. By now the other two boxcars had been opened and the men leaping from them saw their fellows in the argument with the brakeman. Both groups started converging on the bunch around the beleaguered brakeman.

Among the group that had started the argument, arms were being raised and clenched fists waved angrily. The brakeman who was at the center of the argument wasted no time. He took a half step that placed him within striking distance of the nearest man and knocked him down with a quick jab to the jaw.

At once, the hoboes around the brakeman closed in. They backed him against the side of the boxcar. From both sides the other two bands of boes were running now to join the first. Far up at the head of the string, Foxx saw one of the other brakemen hurrying to help his crewmate. Foxx was rising to his feet with the same idea in mind.

Just as he stood up, Foxx spotted the gleam of a white shirt on one of the men among the group of boes that had gotten out of the boxcar near the head of the train. Foxx froze in a half crouch, between standing and sitting. He watched the group's advance until he was sure he was looking at the man he wanted. As the hoboes strung out along the track, running now, Foxx got the clear look he wanted. He was looking at the busboy, no question about it. He sank slowly back to the cupola seat. Accustomed to making split-second decisions, Foxx made one now. Much as he wanted to help the brakeman, his main job came first. He could not afford to let the youth get a clear look at him.

Suddenly the flat report of a pistol shot broke the still air of the desert sunrise. Foxx turned his attention back to the group attacking the brakeman and saw they were backing away from the train. Sterner, his pistol in his hand, stood on top of the boxcar. His lips were moving, he was obviously shouting at the hoboes. Behind the glassed window of the cupola, Foxx could hear the conductor's voice, but could not make out his words.

Whatever Sterner was saying, it was effective, Foxx thought. The group of hoboes that had been clustering around the brakeman were shouting back at Sterner, but the other two bands had stopped and stood at a distance, listening. The brakeman pointed at one of the hoboes in the bunch that stood in front of him. The man began shaking his head, but the others began to draw away from him. Sterner raised his pistol, and the hobo the brakeman had indicated began walking away from the train. He kept looking back, but each time he turned his head the conductor raised his pistol, and the man went on walking.

Slowly, the bindlestiffs who stood under Sterner's

eyes started back to the boxcar from which they'd emerged. Sterner waved his gun, first at one of the other hobo bands, then at the other. They, too, went back to the cars they'd just left.

From the water tower, the locomotive tooted. The brakemen who'd been running to help Sterner hurried back to their stations.

Sterner still stood on top of the boxcar, watching the man he'd driven away from the tracks. The lone figure standing on the alkali flat was watching his companions, who were leaning out of the boxcar doors eyeing the scene.

A shiver ran down the string of boxcars as the tender hit the coupling of the leading car. The brakeman standing ready disappeared between the tender and the boxcar. Moments later the thunking of tightened linking pins began to sound; the engineer was taking the slack out of his train.

Slowly the drag moved forward. Foxx saw the brakemen appear on the cartops. Sterner began walking back along the moving cars, his eyes on the lone hobo, who still stood motionless fifty yards from the tracks. The man made no effort to run and board the train. He was still standing there when the caboose passed him.

Foxx dropped down the ladder to the floor of the caboose as Sterner came in the forward door. He told the conductor, "You did a good job, there. As good as I'd've done, if it'd been my problem."

"Maybe I got away with it because I knew you'd be watching and that I could count on you lending a hand if things got really bad," Sterner said. "Do you know that's the first time I've felt like I had to shoot this gun? Why, I've only had to take it out two or three times before, times when hoboes have been giving me trouble. Most of 'em just melt down when I pull back my coat and let 'em see I've got a pistol on."

"For what it's worth, I'll give you a little advice," Foxx said. "Guns are meant to be used. If you don't have the guts to pull the trigger, you've got no business carrying one."

Sterner nodded, then a worried frown formed on his face. "I hope I didn't interfere with your plans, Mr. Foxx."

"You didn't," Foxx assured him. "I saw the man I'm trailing, so I know he's on the train."

"I thought you knew that all the time."

"I was pretty sure he was. There's considerable difference between that and really knowing."

"I'll tell you something, though," the conductor went on. "If I hadn't known you wanted one of those boes real bad, I'd've left all of 'em back there instead of just the one that hit Flannigan."

"If I hadn't wanted him as bad as I do, I wouldn't've asked you to lock up the cars in the first place," Foxx reminded him. "No, you did the right thing, Sterner. As a matter of fact, you've made my job easier. I'll see you get a good mention in my report."

"Well, I'd like that, of course. But I don't see how I made your job easier."

"You did. I know that fellow's on the train, but he didn't find out that I am. That's going to make it easier for me to track him until he leads me to his friends."

Which, Foxx reminded himself soberly, *might not be as easy as I just made it sound.*

CHAPTER 9

Through the day Number Nine steamed on. The country through which the C&K tracks ran was ever changing. One hour the train would pass through the bleak and darkly forbidding stretches of crusted sands; the next hour the sands would give way to alkali flats as white as fresh snow or to rock outcrops extending from high isolated peaks with flanks covered by pines, which would give way near the desert floor to clumps of gray-green sage.

Foxx went up to the cupola at every water tower and station stop. He saw the busboy only once, just before noon, when the hoboes left their boxcars almost as though their moves had been prearranged. They walked from the stopped cars to the cars to the water tower and while the tender's tank was being filled clustered under the leaking joint between tower and spout to catch the water that spilled out of the loose joint. Some had tin cups or cans, but most of the boes cupped their hands to capture a mouthful or two at a time. Foxx noticed that the fireman handling the spout waited to raise it until all the free-riders had a chance to drink.

Later, when the train had moved on, Foxx asked

Sterner about the incident. The conductor replied, "Well, hell, Mr. Foxx! You can't deny a drink of water to a thirsty man, just because he's a bum. Most train crews I've worked with sorta look the other way when the boes get thirsty enough to come up and drink while the tender's filling."

"I can't say I blame the crews," Foxx said. "And I don't suppose a C&K locomotive could make much steam out of the little bit of water they drink."

It was a long day of slow uphill travel up the mountain spurs the tracks crossed and even slower downhill progress on the steeper grades when the brakemen and conductor turned out to set the brakes and keep the string from gathering slack. The engineer crowded on steam across the flats, but much of the time made up by the fast steaming was canceled by the long waits the freight was forced to make, sitting on siding to leave the main line clear for a westbound freight or passenger train, or for a faster eastbound passenger drag to pass.

There were lunch counters at the two largest stations where they stopped to cut off cars. The crew ate at trackside cafes, and a few of the hoboes who had money bought sandwiches. Those who were flat broke panhandled at the restaurant's back doors. Foxx was unable to leave the caboose, of course. Sterner brought him sandwiches, always thin slices of drying ham or cheese between thick hard-crusted slabs of bread.

Had Number Nine been a passenger train, it would have made a long stop at Carlin, the first division point east of the Sierra, but for freight trains the important station was Elko, twenty miles further east. It was the distribution point for the big silver mines in the vicinity, the Bullion and the Butterfly and several more. At the division point the train stopped only long enough to switch engines and cabooses. Sterner arranged the switch so that Foxx could literally step

from the old caboose to the new one and avoid the
risk of being seen by his quarry.

By the time Number Nine puffed into Elko, nearly
three hundred miles from Nevada's western border,
the scarlet-pink of the desert sunset was fading to
gray. Foxx was beginning to wonder if he'd been mis-
taken about the busboy's destination. Then, when the
string pulled up to a straining stop in the big freight
yards at Elko, he saw what he'd been waiting for. A
white-shirted figure dropped from one of the hobo-oc-
cupied boxcars and hurried across the yards, away
from the train.

Dropping from the cupola, Foxx grabbed his valise
and followed the blob of white through the fast-
deepening darkness. As long as they were in the
freight yards he had no trouble keeping the white
shirt in sight while he trailed a safe distance behind.
The shirt picked up the dim glows from the red and
green switch signals and gave Foxx a gauge not only
of direction but of distance. When they left the yards
behind, Foxx was forced to speed up and stay closer,
to move more cautiously, as he trailed the youth
along the rough ground that began as soon as the
maze of sidings and shunt tracks merged into the
main line.

Foxx's eyes began to adjust to the pitch blackness
of the night as he felt his way with his feet, trying to
keep from making a noise. He could make out nothing but a vague intermittently visible ghost of a blur
in the gloom now, but he hesitated to move closer. If
a misstep drew his quarry's attention, the youth had
only to glance back and Foxx would be silhouetted
against the glow the lights of the yards and town sent
into the dark sky. He frowned as he tried to keep the
moving youth in sight but out of earshot. He remembered nothing east of the town along the C&K line
except—his frown changed to a grin—except the
stockpens, which had been located distant from the

main yards because of their odor and the flies they drew.

Absorbed in his thoughts, Foxx had unconsciously speeded up. He stopped quickly and dropped to the ground when the flare of a match cut the darkness ahead and the figure of the youth was cast for a few seconds in dark silhouette. Then the busboy's voice broke the quiet.

"Stud?" he called, "Stud?" Is that you?"

"No." The reply came from the spot where the match had flared and where the firefly tip of a lighted cigarette now glowed. "Eddie? It's me, Cal. Stud et something that turned his stummick. He's got a bad case of squitters."

"Well, I'm damn glad to see either one of you," the youth replied. "I was afraid you'd get tired of waiting."

Foxx was now sure that Eddie hadn't lied about his name, and he also had a name for the man who'd been waiting for him—Cal. He thought, all I need now is a last name to go with 'em. And there was also a third name to remember—Stud. The pair ahead began talking, Eddie's voice fading a bit as he moved up to the waiting man. Foxx took no chances in trying to steal up closer; he could hear well enough where he was.

Cal said complainingly, "You sure took your damn sweet time getting back. Two nights, now, I've waited. If you hadn't showed up tonight, I was aiming to cut a shuck."

"I couldn't help it, Cal. The damned railroad detectives caught me. They give me a real bad time."

"You didn't spill anything, did you?"

"No. I kept my mouth shut, like we all agreed we would if we got caught. But it wasn't easy to do, I'll tell you that."

"How you get away?" Cal asked.

"It'd take too long to tell you all of it right now.

Come on, Cal! Let's move along! You got a horse for
me, ain't you?"

"Damn it, of course I got you a horse! Why in hell
you think I been waiting?"

"Let's start then. I'll tell you all of it while we're
riding."

Foxx had dropped his valise and drawn his
revolver while the two were arguing. He started to
stand up, but afterthoughts rushed to his mind and
he dropped flat again.

No, he told himself, *it'd be a fool's trick, stopping
these two right now. Elko's not that big a place.
Won't take me long to find out who they are, now
I've got a couple of names to drop here and there.
And there might even be more of them than three
mixed up in this. If that's so, I don't want any of 'em
to get away.*

Holstering his pistol, Foxx lay still. He heard the
light broken-paced hoof thuds of horses being led, followed by the creaking of saddle leather as the two
mounted. Then irregular hoofbeats turned into a
rhythmic drumming as the two men rode off.

Foxx lay flat until the hoofbeats died away, then
picked up his valise and started back toward town.
He was suddenly ravenously hungry. The tension of
the chase had suddenly snapped. For three nights and
three days he'd slept in brief snatches, eaten at odd
times, and except for the few hours he'd spent with
Vida Martin, had focused his full attention on quarry
and pursuit. For the first time in sixty-four hours the
intensity of his concentration could be relaxed, and
he became very aware of his personal needs.

Until the lights of the freight yards were just
ahead, Foxx walked beside the tracks. When he came
to the crisscross of tracks in the yard, he crossed the
single track that ran to the stockpens and walked
along the street. When he reached the big frame
warehouses that towered at one edge of the yards, he

stopped for a breather, set his valise on the ground, and lighted a stogie. With the pungent smoke wreathing his head, he took stock of his surroundings.

Foxx's last case in Elko had been more than two years ago, when the town was still a fresh settlement of raw lumber mushrooming in size. He could see from the lights that spilled out of the buildings ahead that Elko had changed. Unlike the western towns that had grown up slowly, when civilization followed trails and roads, Elko's pattern was like that of later settlements which had followed the new civilization bringer, the railways.

Towns oriented to wagon roads had a main street lined with business buildings, with houses clustered behind them. Most railroad towns were one-sided, with a main street paralleling the railroad tracks and cross streets radiating away from the tracks. Elko was one of the few railroad towns that had two main streets, one on each side of the tracks. In the approximate center of town stood the passenger depot; a hotel—the Depot Hotel, Foxx recalled—stood close to the depot, between the tracks and one of the parallel main streets. The big warehouses had been built as temporary storage for the mining machinery and equipment that was the C&K's principal load. Intersecting streets, some of them crossing the tracks, were lined with dwellings.

Looking along the street, Foxx could see only three things that interested him. The first was the batwing doors of a saloon just ahead. The other was the sign "Cafe" on the windows of a building further down the street. The third was the sign on the Depot Hotel. He headed first for the saloon.

There were only three customers in the barnlike building, all of them at the far end of the long bar, and a single barkeeper was on duty. The poker tables in the rear of the bar were idle and unlighted, not even a house dealer waiting for enough customers to form a game. The battered piano that stood against the wall opposite the bar was silent. Foxx studied the array of bottles on the backbar. Few of them had labels. He decided that no matter what label was on the bottle from which a drink was poured, he'd be getting raw, unaged keg whiskey.

"What's your pleasure, mister?" the chubby barkeep asked, eyeing Foxx's valise and the twisted stogie that was clamped between his lips without bothering to hide his curiosity.

"Beer. Cold, and out of a bottle, if you've got it."

"Colorado or California?"

"Make it Colorado." Foxx watched the barkeep pour the beer. The man was as interested in peering covertly at Foxx as he was in keeping too much head from bubbling up in the stein. Seeing that conversation was inevitable, Foxx remarked, "It's a quiet night."

"Always is, this time of week. If you're still in town, drop by on Saturday. You'll see plenty of action then." The barkeep pushed the stein across to Foxx, ignoring the silver dollar that Foxx had placed on the mahogany. "We've got games and girls both then. And a piano player, too."

"And the hands from the ranches, I expect."

"Oh, sure. About the only time we get a crowd now. Not like it was when the C&K was laying track a few years back." With a trace of bitterness in his voice, the man added. "Most of the trade between Saturdays goes to the station lunch counter. But it don't amount to all that much, just passengers getting off to stretch their legs or get a bite during stopovers."

Foxx took a swallow of the beer. It trickled down his throat, cold and tangy, washing away the layer of coal dust that had been deposited during the trip. The thought occurred to him that the place at which Ed and Cal had arranged to meet might not be too far from the saloon. Concluding that a stab in the dark could do no harm, and might open a trail he could follow to the identities of the pair, he took the stein from his lips and keeping his voice carefully casual, said, "Too bad. I was hoping I'd see Cal or Eddie, or maybe both of them, in town tonight."

"That'd be the Becker boys, I guess?" The barkeep looked up and saw that Foxx was sipping his beer again. Without waiting for a reply, he went on, "You just missed Cal; he was in here last night and earlier this evening, too. I can't say about Eddie. He hasn't dropped in for a spell."

"Cal looked good and healthy, I hope?"

"Same as always."

Foxx didn't want to make his interest in Cal and Eddie too obvious, now that he'd learned their family name. Besides that, any more questions might lead to a slip that would reveal he had no knowledge of them other than their first names. He drained the stein and put it down.

"Another one?" the barkeep asked.

"Not till after supper and I'm ready for a night-cap."

"Sorry. We don't spread a free lunch except on the nights we're busy. Come in Saturday, and help yourself. And come back after supper for that nightcap."

"I just might." The barkeeper's suggestion reminded Foxx that he'd be spending the night in the Depot Hotel, and that like all railroad hotels it would not have a saloon attached. He said, "Tell you what, friend. You reach me a bottle of Cyrus Noble with the seal still on it from your backbar there, and I'll have my nightcap at the hotel."

For a moment the barkeep looked angrily at Foxx, then his lips split in a grin. "You know your mind, don't you, mister?" He selected a bottle from the backbar shelves and held it out for Foxx to inspect. Foxx nodded and replaced the dollar that still lay on the bar with a five-dollar gold piece. While the barkeep made change, Foxx tucked the bottle in his already-full valise. The barkeep handed Foxx his change.

"How's the café up the street?" Foxx asked, pocketing the money.

Pursing his lips, the man shook his head. "If you like good whiskey, I'd say you like good food. That place is a Chinee joint. All you'll get is rice and chicken. Go on up the street to that café past the Depot Hotel."

"Thanks for the tip." Fox picked up his valise. "I'll be in again real soon. You serve your beer the way it ought to be, good and cold, but not too cold to freeze out the taste."

"Wait a minute! You want me to tell Cal who it was asking for him?"

"Oh, I'll see him when he comes in on Saturday. It's not all that important. All I wanted to do was pass the time of day with him while I'm in town."

Before the barkeep could ask any more questions, Foxx left. There were only a few people on the street, and the stores he looked into as he passed were as bare of patrons as the saloon had been. The thought of food made Foxx walk faster. He glanced across the street at the Depot Hotel as he passed it, saw only two windows lighted on its second floor, and deduced that he wouldn't have any trouble getting a room. The C&K, he thought, certainly wasn't going to make much of a profit out of its hotel in Elko. The restaurant he came to further down the street looked only a bit more inviting than the first, but by this time he was too hungry to care.

Surprisingly, he got an unremarkable but quite edible meal of soup, steak, onions, potatoes, pie, and coffee. Food made the night look a bit brighter. After he'd finished a second cup of coffee and had a stogie glowing, Foxx felt ready for anything. Standing in front of the restaurant, he surveyed the street. While he'd been eating, the stores had closed. Except for the second saloon a few doors from the restaurant, everything was dark and shuttered.

Swinging his valise jauntily, Foxx strolled back in the direction of the station. He could see that the other main street, across the tracks, was deserted and its stores closed, too. With a shrug he gave up the idea he'd had of a stroll before bedtime to stretch his legs after the long hours of sitting in a caboose. He arrived at the C&K station, where only a night-light glowed. A few dozen yards beyond the station the ornately scrolled facade of the Depot Hotel offered the only haven that attracted him. Foxx gave in and started toward it.

Lights were still showing from one or two of the windows on the second floor, but when Foxx went into the lobby only a single turned-down lamp broke the gloom. He saw a push bell on the registration desk with a sign inviting latecomers to ring for service. Foxx tapped the bell, and after a few moments a much-corseted woman appeared through a door behind the desk.

"If it's a room you want, I can give you a nice one on the corner, on the second floor," she said. "No loud noise or fighting and no carousing. This is a temperance house, so you won't be kept awake by a lot of noise from a saloon," she said in one breath, looking somewhere in the air over Foxx's head.

Foxx took his wallet from his breast pocket and flipped it open to show his railroad badge. The woman inspected it closely. When she looked up at Foxx, he could tell she was impressed.

"Well, my goodness!" she exclaimed. "From the main office in San Francisco, I suppose, Mr. Foxx?" When Foxx nodded, she continued, "You're welcome, I'm sure. I don't see many of you men from there, mostly the ones from the head office stay at the divi-

sion point. How long will you be staying, Mr. Foxx?
Not that it matters, seeing how slow business is right
now. I'm Mrs. Fogarty, and if you'll just sign the register, you can go right on upstairs and get to bed.
Bathroom's at the end of the hall. I'll put you in
room 21. I guess you know the depot's got a
lunchroom here you can eat. If there's—"

Foxx despaired of ever hearing an end to the landlady's continuous chatter. He interrupted its flow.
"Thank you, Mrs. Fogarty. I'll be here a few days.
And if it's all the same to you, I won't sign your register." He dropped his voice. "Confidential railroad
business. I'm sure you understand. Now, if you'll just
give me the key—"

"Oh, of course." The landlady was flustered—
whether by his remark about confidential business or
just by the thought of having someone from the mysterious main office stopping there, Foxx couldn't tell.
She took a key off one of the hooks set into the wall
behind the desk and handed it to him. "Now, get a
good night's rest, Mr. Foxx. If there's anything you
want—"

"Thanks, Mrs. Fogarty." As Foxx turned away
from the desk, a garishly lithographed poster tacked
to the wall near the entrance door caught his attention. It depicted a hot-air balloon sailing at an impos-
sibly high altitude above a crowd of spectators while
a woman in tights hung by her toes from a trapeze
below the balloon's wicker basket. The legend pro-
claimed:

DARING BALLOON ASCENSION! ! DEATH
DEFYING ACROBATICS HIGH IN THE
SKY! ! MADAM ASUZA, AERIAL ARTISTE, PER-
FORMS! !

Below the printed legend, someone had written a
date—only four days hence, Foxx noted—in heavy
crayon.

Mrs. Fogarty said breathlessly, "Isn't it exciting,

Mr. Foxx! Why, there's never been anything like that here! Just imagine, sailing through the air like a bird! And a young lady doing it, too. Think of it!"

"To tell the truth, I don't think so much of it," Foxx replied. "There's some things that aren't natural for humans to do, and sailing through the air's one of 'em."

"Well!" a woman's voice broke in. "Spoken like a true fogy! Not too long ago, people were saying the same thing about railway trains, that moving at such speed would take a person's breath away and kill them! And before that a lot of people didn't think the world was round! Not natural, indeed!"

Foxx had turned when the woman first started speaking, and stood watching her with his mouth open while she stood on the stairs and continued her tirade. He said, "Now, if I've offended you, ma'am, I beg your pardon. But you've got to agree some things just don't fit in with nature's schemes."

"And you believe that going off the ground is one of them?" she demanded.

"I can't truthfully say. I guess it's something you'd have to get used to. But the way I feel right now, I'll go just as high up in the air as I can while I still keep one foot on the ground."

"Meaning, I suppose, that anybody willing to take both feet off the ground is foolish?" she asked icily.

Mrs. Fogarty broke in. "Now, I'm sure Mr. Foxx didn't intend to offend you, madam," she said placatingly. Then when Foxx and the newcomer stood silent, the landlady added, "Madam Asuza, this is Mr. Foxx, from the railroad's main office in San Francisco."

Foxx managed to say, "I'm truly sorry, Madam Asuza. I guess I put my foot in my mouth, didn't I?"

Madam Asuza came the rest of the way down the stairs. She moved lightly on her feet, almost like she was dancing, Foxx thought. She stood beside Foxx, almost as tall as he was.

"You're not the only one who feels that people ought to keep one foot on the ground," she said. There was no anger in her voice now, as she stood looking at Foxx. "I suppose I ought not have scolded you the way I did. But it's been a tiring day, and my nerves are a little edgy."

"Oh, you did right to stand up to me," Foxx told. "I guess ballooning's something that's coming on us sooner or later. But I'm satisfied to keep on riding the train."

"That's your choice, of course," she replied. She turned to Mrs. Fogarty. "I was walking down the hall and I heard you talking. I thought perhaps my manager had gotten here at last with my balloon."

Foxx studied the aerialist. She was small and slightly built, her body that of an adolescent girl, but her features and bust were those of a ripely mature woman. Her blond hair was not worn in the upsweep puff that was the current fashion but in a loose coil at the nape of her neck. Her eyes were dark brown, her nose perhaps a bit too sharp, her lips pouting and full. The light blue silk kimona that was wrapped around her, belted with a wide sash, fell from bulging breasts to a slim waist and narrow hips.

Mrs. Fogarty said, "No. He hasn't come in, yet. Don't worry though, Madam Asuza, he'll get here in plenty of time. Maybe on the Flyer; it'll be passing through in just a little while now."

Madam Asuza sighed. "It's just that there's so much to do! It takes us two or three days to get everything ready."

Foxx said, "It's none of my business, but if there's something the C&K's to blame for, your gear not getting here, maybe I can help."

"Mr. Foxx is from the main office in San Francisco," Mrs. Fogarty repeated.

Madam Asuza turned to face Foxx. "If you could only find out whether it's on the way! Or if it's not, where it's located!"

"Well, that oughtn't be too hard to do. Not tonight, of course. But if you'll have breakfast with me in the morning, and tell me about your trouble, I'll be glad to make up for belittling your work and see what I can do."

"I'd be very grateful, Mr.—Mr. Foxx. What time?"

"Well, the depot'll be open about seven. If that's not too early."

"No time's too early for me, the way things are now. Shall we meet here in the lobby, then?"

"It'll be my pleasure, Madam Asuza." Foxx watched the aerialist go back up the stairs, struck again by the lightness of her steps.

Mrs. Fogarty said, "She's a very nice young lady, Mr. Foxx, no matter about the kind of work she does. Goodness! I wouldn't be brave enough to fly, I'm sure. I do hope you can find her balloon. She's been worried ever since she got here this morning."

"I'll do whatever I can," Foxx promised. "Now I'm ready to go to bed myself. Good night, Mrs. Fogarty."

In his room, Foxx poured a drink and lighted a stogie. He sipped and puffed thoughtfully while he took off his dusty suit and draped it across a chair. He tried to put his mind on what he'd learned by listening at the stockpens and later at the saloon, but his train of thought was interrupted by his memory of Madam Asuza's strange girl-woman face. He swallowed the last of the whiskey and dropped the butt of his stogie in the cuspidor. The bed suddenly looked very inviting. He stepped out of his singlet and crawled between the sheets. He was asleep almost as soon as his head touched the pillow.

CHAPTER 10

Foxx snapped awake. The windows across from the bed showed as gray oblongs in the still-dark room. Though he was sure he hadn't overslept, he reached over to the bedside table where his gold hunter-cased repeater lay beside his holstered revolver. The tiny musical tinkling that broke the stillness when he pressed the chime lever told him it was five o'clock.

Foxx frowned, then his face cleared. His watch was set on C&K time in San Francisco, and the C&K was one of a majority of railroads that—even before its formal approval by Congress—had adopted the long-debated plan of dividing the country into standardized time zones an hour apart from east to west. In Elko it was six o'clock, and he had all the time he needed.

Leaning over the edge of the bed and looking under it, Foxx saw what he'd expected, a chamber pot. He used it, then took a quick whore's bath. Filling his cupped palm with whiskey, he rubbed down his torso, rinsed with water from the pitcher on the washstand to remove the fine, clinging train soot the whiskey had loosened, then rubbed down with the coarse huck towel that hung on the stand's end.

A brisk shaking dislodged most of the dust and soot

from his suit. Foxx took a fresh shirt from his valise, putting an unopened bundle of stogies on the table as he rummaged in the bag. He donned the shirt and his trousers and sat down on the bed to pull on his boots. Still sitting there, he snapped the narrow cloth strips that held the short crooked cigars twisted together and lighted one. Tilting the whiskey bottle, he took an eye-opening swallow and puffed on the cigar, relishing the blending of the pungent liquor and equally pungent cigar smoke on his tastebuds.

Tucking his black cravat into a coat pocket, Foxx walked briskly across the street to the only building that showed a light at this early hour, the barbershop. Fifteen minutes later, his face still tingling from the bay rum and feeling satisfactorily smooth to his fingertips, his cravat neatly looped, he crossed the street to the hotel.

Madam Asuza was just coming down the stairway. Foxx looked at her approvingly. She wore a tan gabardine suit with a dark brown velour collar, a white scarf wrapped around her neck and its ends tucked behind the coat lapels. The suit had obviously been tailored to her slight but voluptuous figure.

"Good morning, Mr. Foxx. I hope I haven't kept you waiting."

Foxx swept off his Borsalino and bowed. "Not a minute, Madam Asuza. I just got here myself. I don't suppose the shipment you're so concerned about was on the Flyer last night?"

"No. I woke up whenever a train passed, and waited, but Cap didn't show up. And I'm really worried as much about him getting here as I am about the equipment."

Foxx held the door for her; they stepped outside, and she took his arm. He led the way across the street, saying, "I don't know whether the depot lunchroom's open yet, but I think we'd be better off going to that restaurant"—he pointed with his free hand—"than eating at the depot."

"Yes," she smiled. "I've been eating there because I haven't wanted to get too far from the hotel, in case Cap got here."

They reached the restaurant and ordered. While they were waiting, Foxx asked. "Where's your equipment coming from, Madam Asuza?"

"Laramie was our last show. The balloon got torn, and Cap stayed behind to get it fixed while I came on ahead. But he was supposed to leave the next day. He should've been here by now. And even if the equipment got here, I couldn't do an ascension without Cap."

"Your helper?"

"Oh—manager is what we call him. He arranges the bookings, and inflates the bag and launches it. Then he follows me in a wagon on the ground in case the balloon drifts. Which it does almost always."

Foxx had been thinking. "Laramie'd be the U.P. Your man and balloon would've got onto the C&K over a connecting spur out of Ogden. Have you wired Laramie, Madam Asuza?"

"No. And please don't call me by that silly name. It was the name that was already on the posters we bought. My name's Joyce Kilpatrick, Mr. Foxx. And I suppose you know that people in my line of work aren't much on formality. Please, call me Joyce."

"If that's what you'd like." Foxx hesitated and added, "I'd feel better using your first name if you'd drop the mister."

"Surely you have a first name? Everybody has to have one."

"Oh, sure. But I don't answer to it so good because nobody ever calls me anything but Foxx." The waiter set platters of ham and eggs before them and poured coffee. Foxx said, "Well, I can't answer for the U.P., of course, but if your stuff's been mislaid anyplace along the C&K, I'll sure find out about it."

"I certainly hope you can find it in time. We've already collected an advance payment from the hotel—"

Foxx interrupted her. "Hold on. You mean the Depot Hotel?"

"Oh, my no! The one just south of town. The Humboldt Spa, or Sulpha Hotel, or whatever they call it."

"You mean the one down by the hothole. Sure." Fox tended to forget the resort that had been famous long before the railroad came to Elko and made access to it easier. The Humboldt Sulpher Hotel was almost as well known as the bigger spa at Steamboat Hot Springs, in spite of its isolation. He asked Joyce, "How come you're not stopping out there, then, instead of right here in town?"

"I just intended to stay at the Depot Hotel until Cap and the equipment got here," Joyce said. "But as you see, I'm still stuck, and so is my balloon."

"Well, don't feel so bad, Joyce. I'll try my best to dig it up for you."

"You don't know how grateful I'll be." Joyce looked around and dropped her voice as she confessed, "The trouble is that if we don't make the ascension when we agreed we would, three days from today, we'll have to refund the advance money the hotel's paid us. And—well, the truth is, we don't have the money to refund it. So you see I don't have much time to spare."

"That makes it real serious," Foxx agreed. "I can see that. Well, Joyce, stop worrying now and eat your breakfast. I'll have some news for you by noon, maybe earlier."

They finished breakfast in virtual silence. Joyce was too downcast, Foxx thought, for him to try to take her mind off her troubles with idle chatter. He walked with her back to the hotel, then went to the depot. A grill-enclosed partition divided the interior from the lunchroom with its curved counter, and scattered tables took up the remaining space. A stairway rose along the back walls. A few breakfasters were in the lunchroom area, a long ticket counter was behind the grille, and the chatter of a telegraph key sounded from the end wall.

Foxx went up the stairs. At the end of the corridor leading from the top, a sign read, "Robert Scott, Stationmaster." Foxx entered without knocking. A young-old man sat behind the desk in the center of the office. He was concentrating so thoroughly on the papers spread before him that he did not appear to hear Foxx open and close the door. He wore the blue-serge vest and trousers which most railroaders preferred and carried the badge of the profession, a heavy gold watch chain draped across his unbuttoned vest.

"If you're too busy, I can come back later," Foxx said.

"No. I'll be with you—" For the first time, Scott looked up. His face broke into a grin. "Foxx! What the devil's taken you away from the city? I hope it's not trouble in our division."

As they shook hands across the desk, Foxx replied, "Well, it is and it's not." He pulled up a chair and sat down without being asked; Foxx and Scott went back to the days when Foxx was running down a gang of train robbers in southern Nebraska and Scott had been the stationmaster, ticket agent, freight agent, dispatcher and sole C&K employee at the little tanktown station where the chase had ended. Foxx went on, "I guess you heard about somebody trying to blow up our line, in the bay area."

"Yes. We were lucky. Or you were—I hear you pulled the fuse in time."

"And you heard about the man who tried to shoot Caleb Petersen being tied up with the dynamiter?"

Scott's jaw dropped. "Caleb shot? When? There hasn't been anything about that come over the wire!"

"Well," Foxx said drily, "it didn't happen on C&K property. And I didn't say he was hit. He was shot at, that's all." At the same time, Foxx wondered whether it had been Caleb or Jim Flaherty who'd put the lid on the news of the shooting.

Scott said, frowning, "You being here doesn't mean that you're looking for dynamite trouble in this division, does it?"

"No. I think this is too close to where he lives."

"Sounds to me like you've got a line on him."

"A pretty thin one, right now." Foxx lighted up a stogie. "There's more than one man mixed up in this mess, Bob. Now, I'm going to tell you some things I don't want talked about. Not to anybody, and that includes the division super."

"I was wondering why you came to Elko instead of stopping at the division point. All right. I'm mum. Go ahead."

"You know anything about a family named Becker that lives someplace close around here?"

"Sure. Why—" Scott's eyes popped wide. "My God! Freddie Becker! Damn it, aren't we ever going to hear the last of him?"

"Wait a minute." Foxx frowned. "I'm talking about Eddie and Cal Becker. Who in hell is Freddie?"

"Freddie's the dead brother." Seeing Foxx's frown, Scott explained. "There were four Becker boys, Foxx. Stud, Cal, Eddie, and Freddie. The family's got a horse ranch down along the Humboldt River, southeast of town. There's Mrs. Becker, too, and a sister. Her name's Rose."

"I'd guess Mrs. Becker's a widow woman, since you didn't say anything about the boys' daddy."

"That's right. He was killed in the war. The Beckers got here a long time before the C&K did, Foxx. They migrated out of—well, if I ever knew where, I've forgotten. Kentucky, West Virginia. Someplace back in that part of the East. It seems to me somebody said he was a horse trader or a horse trainer before he went into the army."

"So the boys just come by it naturally."

"I guess that's the way of it. They round up wild

mustangs and break 'em about halfway, then ship them to cattle country. Texas, Wyoming, Montana, places like that."

"Can they still make a go of mustanging, Bob?"

"Oh, sure. There's plenty of wild horses. The ranchers say mustangs can get fat off what a herd of sheep leaves."

"Right now I want to hear about Freddie Becker. He was killed, you said. Would I be right in guessing it was a C&K train that killed him?"

"You'd be right on the mark."

"Was it his fault or the engineer's?"

"Oh, hell, Foxx, you know how it is with a train accident. Whose fault it is depends on who's telling about it."

"And the way the Beckers tell it, Freddie wasn't to blame?"

"What you'd imagine, isn't it? From what I remember, he was driving a mustang herd through one of our cuts this side of the Humboldt. The Flyer whistled the bridge, and the horses panicked. Freddie was in the middle of the bunch, trying to quiet them down. Maybe he could've gotten free, maybe not. Anyhow, the engine plowed into them, and Freddie got his."

"But he could've pulled away from the herd?"

"I think he could. But the Beckers never admitted it. I guess Freddie was Ma Becker's special pet, being the youngest."

"Which one's the oldest?"

"That'd be Stud. His name's Anse, short for Ansel, I think. But everybody calls him Stud."

"Who's next in line? Eddie or Cal?"

"Cal. Not that it makes much difference which Becker you point at. They're all mean and stubborn as mules. They come from feuding country, Foxx. I know. I spent a little time in those hills where they started, when I was breaking in, on the B&O. People there hand grudge fights on down in the family, year after year. They don't know how to say quit."

"So I've heard. And the way it looks to me right now, the Beckers are feuding with the C&K."

"Yes." Scott was silent for a moment, then said, "I suppose that ought to've occurred to me when Calhoun came looking for a job here. That was about a year after Freddie got killed."

"Hold up a minute, Bob. You mean you had one of the boys on the C&K payroll?"

"I'm afraid so. Not for very long, but he did work here."

Foxx lighted a fresh stogie and settled back in his chair. "You'd better tell me about it."

"There's not a lot to tell. After the accident had blown over pretty much, Cal came looking for work. It surprised me some, but I took it to mean that they were looking to get some money out of the road, one way or another."

"So you put him on."

"Not right away. Not until he'd been back pestering me four or five times. Now, you know how railroads break men in, Foxx." Foxx nodded, but Scott had already started ticking off the job ladder that a man must climb. "Callboy or swampie first, and if they stand up to that, section hand or maybe car toad. Then yardman, switchman, on up the line. Well, that didn't strike Cal's fancy, so finally I put him on as a handler down at the shipping pens. It was something he could do, and got him out from underfoot. It was in the back of my mind, too, that hiring him might settle their bad feelings, and if I kept turning him away I might be stirring up the old trouble."

"Um-humm," Foxx grunted. "I can guess from there on, Bob. He held onto the job awhile, probably spent a lot of his time hanging around places he didn't have any business being, asking questions, getting in the way. So you fired him."

"You've called it up to a point. I didn't fire him. I was just getting ready to, but he quit."

"That was how long ago?"

"Seven months, maybe eight."

"But he'd worked here long enough to find out how a railroad's run, long enough to know how to hit back at us for his brother being killed. Even if it wasn't our fault."

Scott nodded. "It didn't occur to me until right now that Cal had that in mind when he came looking for a job. And when I heard about the dynamite business the other day, I never did think about the Beckers. Can you pin the dynamite setting on Cal, Foxx?"

"Not with the little bit I've got now. Eddie trying to shoot Caleb, that's another thing. There were plenty of witnesses to what he did."

"So you're sure it was Eddie Becker."

"Certain sure, even if I didn't have a name to put on him until last night. Then I heard him and Cal talking, and weaseled their names out of a barkeep in a saloon down by the stockpens."

"You trailed Eddie here? All the way from San Francisco?" Scott's surprise showed in his voice.

"Sure. It wasn't at all hard. I just about had to. I tried to drag some information out of him, but he acted like his jaws were wired shut. Are all the Beckers as stubborn as he is, Bob?"

"They're all of a kind. Hardheaded and with a streak of meanness as wide as the stripes on a polecat's back."

"Well, if you can't crack a hard nut with a nutcracker, you can always use a hammer."

Scott said thoughtfully, "Where does Stud fit into things? He'd be the one I'd've named to set the dynamite. He's the meanest of the three."

"It could've been him, for all I know. Or he could be the one I traded shots with in the dark. It had to be him or Cal. I know it wasn't Eddie."

His voice worried, Scott warned Foxx, "They won't give up, you know. And that bothers me, because they might dynamite the tracks right around here."

"Oh, they'll try again, all right. Dynamiters just keep on blowing things up, or trying to, until they're caught. That's why I figure I haven't got much time to waste."

"What do you plan to do?"

"Stop 'em, of course. I don't know exactly how yet, but I'll figure something out."

"Can I help?"

"That's one reason I'm here. I want you to handle whatever messages I have to send the San Francisco office. Every damn dispatcher I ever saw spends more time swapping gossip with his key than he does sending company messages. So you send my messages yourself and wait to handle the answers. If you haven't forgotten how to punch a key, that is."

"Don't worry, I haven't lost my fist."

"Good. If there's any evidence against the Becker brothers, it'll be at their ranch. I'll have to find out where it is, and I'll need a horse and saddle gear. A rifle, too."

"You can't go after the Beckers by yourself, Foxx!" Scott hesitated and stared at his friend. "Unless you just plan to go out and shoot them out of ambush. And that's not your style."

"No. I'm a detective, Bob. Not a hired killer. I want the three of 'em in court, and I need evidence. Going out to their ranch and nosying around is the only way I'll find it."

"You'll be taking on three-to-one odds, Foxx! Don't be a fool!" Foxx did not reply, just stared at him, and Scott shook his head. "You're as stubborn as the Beckers, damn it! All right. The C&K's got some horses out in the stockpens, and saddle gear, of course. And there's a stand of Model '66 Winchesters in one of the warehouses, left over from the time we got ready for Paiute trouble."

"Fresh ammunition, I hope?"

"Not very. But you can get what you need in town. We've got maps that'll get you to the Becker ranch easier than I can tell you how to find it. It's not far, just over a half-day's ride, southeast of town, along Lazy Creek. I'll tell my clerk—"

Foxx broke in. "No. No clerks, Bob. You get out the maps yourself."

"Sure. It slipped my mind, what you said a minute ago. I won't forget it again, though."

"Now, there's one other thing," Foxx told him. "This one hasn't got anything to do with the Beckers."

"Well, that'll be a change. What is it?"

"There's a pretty little lady over at the Depot Hotel just about to bust out in tears because her balloon's got mislaid someplace between Laramie and here. How about a push on your brass-pounder to find out about it?"

"Oh, damn it! The balloon! I guess I'm getting old—that slipped my mind, too. Your young lady wouldn't be Madam something or other, would it?"

"Asuza. That's her."

"Well, you can take the message over, I intended to send my clerk with it just when you walked in. The balloon and somebody named Cap will be here on Number Six. It'll be on the siding at noon."

"That'll make her right happy, Bob." Foxx stood up. "If I'm going to ride out to Becker's today, I better go get on some clothes that'll be better in a saddle than these city things. You think you can get my gear together in the next hour or so?"

"Easy enough. But I still hate to see you starting out to the Becker place alone."

Foxx said soberly, "I've said this to you before, Bob. When push comes to shove, there's things a man's got to do himself. You get my gear together. I'll worry about the Beckers."

CHAPTER 11

Foxx resisted the temptation to urge his horse to a faster gait. He was already irritated by the delays he'd encountered before he'd been able to start from Elko, and after being out of the saddle for several months the uneven terrain of the Ruby Mountains foothills was almost as hard on him as it was on the rawboned claybank gelding he rode. Since he'd crossed the Humboldt River just below the railroad bridge and headed southeast, paralleling the mountain crests, the going had gotten progressively rougher.

For every stretch of level ground there had been ten gullies and two or three valleys and at least nine steep ridges that had to be crossed. Some of the gullies were only a foot or so deep, others would have swallowed a half-dozen horsemen. The walls of some of the valleys had been too steep for the horse to manage; he'd had to ride along their rims until the crevasses narrowed to slits that could be crossed. One or two of the ridges had risen with faces as sheer as a masonry wall, and these, too, he'd been forced to circle.

Foxx lurched in the saddle as the claybank's hoof

slid off a flat tilting rock. He reined in and dismounted.

"If the rest of the way's as rough as it's been so
far," he said to the clear empty air, "I won't get back
to town in time for supper."

Taking out the map Bob Scott had given him,
Foxx studied it again. He'd been setting his course by
the sun and by the tip of Ruby Dome, which cut the
sky to his left. Now the sun was directly overhead.
There was no need to consult his watch.

"Noon," he muttered. "And the Becker place still
another twelve miles away."

From the way he read the map, spread on the gelding's rump, Foxx's best guess was that since leaving
the river he'd covered about six miles as a crow might
fly, and that to make those six miles he'd ridden at
least ten. Folding the map and putting it back in his
pocket, Foxx took a meager swallow of water from
the canteen that hung on the saddlehorn and lighted
a stogie. When it was glowing and the sharp-edged
smoke had exerted its soothing effect, he swung into
the saddle again and toed the gelding ahead.

Foxx had started from Elko a lot later than he'd
planned. After leaving Scott's office, he'd gone to the
hotel to tell Joyce Kilpatrick that her balloon and
helper were on their way and that she could quit
worrying. Joyce's gush of relieved thanks and her re-
cital of her immediate plans had kept Foxx immobile
for a half hour. He'd lost more time changing from
his city clothing into jeans and a denim shirt and putting on his heavy boots. When he returned to the depot there'd been another wait for the horse and gear
to be brought up from the stockpens, but he'd put
that delay to good use by studying the map Scott had
dug up.

After that, Foxx had gone back to the hotel to stow
into his saddlebags the necessities that a seasoned
western traveler took with him on any trip of uncer-

tain duration. He'd tucked into the bags a spare pair
of socks and his light wool shirt, a supply of stogies,
matches in a small oilskin pouch, and a box of cartridges for his revolver. As an afterthought after belt-
ing on his Smith & Wesson, Foxx had wrapped the
bottle of whiskey in his longjohns and added it to the
bags.

Finally he'd stopped at the general store across
Commercial Street from the hotel and bought a box
of ammunition for the Winchester. Though the rifle
and his revolver were both .44 caliber, the Winchester
required rimfire cartridges and his Smith & Wesson
was chambered for centerfire cases. Foxx also bought
some strips of venison jerky and a small sack of
parched corn, iron rations that needed no cooking
and would keep him from going hungry in an
emergency.

When Foxx had at last headed east along the Humboldt River, he rode with the satisfying knowledge
that the articles he'd added to the tarpaulin-wrapped
blanket lashed behind his borrowed saddle made him
self-sustaining for an indefinite time. If events made it
necessary, he could stay out in the rough Nevada
range country for months without having to visit a
town and replenish his supplies or equipment.

Foxx had forgotten the contrary character of the
high Nevada foothill country through which he rode.
It was part desert, part grassland, part forest. The
dark green of pines began on the sides of the mountains where winter snows collected and drifted, and
there were pines in the valleys where creeks ran at
the bottom of narrow valleys. Below the mountains,
patches of grassland carpeted some of the valleys,
those where the soil was free from the alkali that
turned so much of the foothill country into barren
soil where only sagebrush could survive. Where the
earth was heavily alkaline not even sagebrush grew;

these places were barren of vegetation, rock-strewn and desolate.

Broad high mesas and small buttes topped with flat sandstone plates rose above flat barren expanses with no apparent reason and no discernible pattern. These were the products of the constant winds, which swept the land during the hot days of summer and stripped the dry sandy soil away from subsurface rock formations, carved the stone itself in ridges and bands, and left upthrust from the flats that which was too heavy to be blown away.

For the next two miles the ground was relatively unbroken, and Foxx made good time. Then the land sloped down to a creek; Paiute Creek, Foxx thought, summoning back the lines he'd seen on the map before putting it away. If the little silver stream that he could see coursing along the valley floor was indeed Paiute Creek, that meant he had only two more streams ahead. The third would be Lazy Creek, which he intended to follow to the Becker ranch. With any luck he'd have two hours or more of daylight left to scout the place before making plans that should let him return to Elko the next day with two, or maybe all three, of the Becker brothers in his custody.

At the streamside Foxx stopped to let the horse drink and rest. He nibbled some shavings of jerky and chewed a few kernels of the corn. He washed the food down with several scanty swallows of water from the creek, and topped off his canteen, more to wet down its felted coating than because the canteen was low. Evaporation from the wet felt would keep the water from getting unpleasantly tepid in the beating sunshine. Remounting, Foxx rode on.

He'd covered what he estimated to be about half the remaining distance to the Becker place and was just guiding the claybank up the sloping side of the last stream before reaching Lazy Creek when he saw the dust smudge rolling into the air above the shoulder of a butte that thrust up from the level land a few miles ahead. A dust cloud that size could mean three or four things, Foxx thought. Most likely, he mused, it was a sheepherder moving a flock out of grazed-over range. It could be a party of late emigrants who hadn't wanted or couldn't afford to move by rail, and had chosen the longer but less expensive method that early emigrants had used, wagons on the old Overland Trail. It could be a Western Union crew out replacing wire; the commercial telegraph line ran south at that point, angling southwest to Virginia City and the Comstock Lode. It could be mustangers, like the Becker brothers.

"Hell," Foxx muttered as he reined in, "it might even be the Becker boys moving one of their horse herds, for all I know."

Even though Foxx at once dismissed his last thought as being too fanciful, he remembered he was nearing the Becker ranch. Dismounting to keep from being silhouetted against the rim of the slope, he stood watching.

Soon the growing size of the dustcloud made it apparent to Foxx that it was not created by a single wagon or even a wagon train. The roiling red dust moved along the butte to the point where the upthrust strip of land dipped sharply to merge with the level ground. A horseman appeared, half lighted, half silhouetted in the angling afternoon sunlight.

Foxx frowned. Perhaps his thought about the Beckers hadn't been so farfetched after all. The distance and the light were not too great for him to recognize Eddie Becker.

He wasted no more time in looking, but led the gelding down the slope until he and the horse were hidden. Wherever Eddie was, Foxx was sure that one or both of the other brothers would be, too. When he was sure that the rising slope concealed him, Foxx left the horse and belly-crawled back up to a point where he could watch. He left his hat behind and shielded his eyes Comanche style, his fingers and palm cupped above his eyebrows in an arch, his thumbs braced on his jawbone. In the shade of his hands, his pupils expanded and sharpened his vision.

Eddie Becker was swinging his horse around now, as the leaders of the mustang herd emerged from behind the butte. Through the dust their unshod hooves stirred up, Foxx could see the dim figure of another rider on the far side of the herd. He watched to see which way the horses would move, ready to shift his own position if the herders turned them his way.

By now the entire herd, about sixty head, had come into sight. In a moment the drag rider appeared. He was far enough behind the mustangs for the freshening breeze the late afternoon was bringing to clear away the dust in front of him. Foxx focused his eyes on the rider and blinked with surprise. If he hadn't seen Eddie Becker in the lead of the herd, he'd have sworn that it was Eddie who was riding drag. Foxx wondered if the flank rider, whose face he hadn't been able to see, had the same strong family resemblance.

While he waited for the mustang herd to pass, Foxx began to plan his next moves. Trailing the herd would be easy. The mustangs would leave a track that even a tenderfoot could follow in the dark. A trail herd could move only half as fast as a single rider, so if the Beckers were headed for Elko to ship out their mustangs, they'd have to spend at least one night in camp. Two of the brothers would almost certainly sleep while the third rode nightherd. Stealing up on the nightherder and taking him without rousing the other two, then surprising the others while they slept, would cancel the three-to-one odds that worked on the Beckers' side during daylight.

Foxx studied the plan for a while, then shook his

head regretfully when he saw its flaw. Simply capturing the brothers would not be enough. Only in Eddie's case was there evidence enough to make a case in court. There was nothing to prove that Cal or Stud Becker had attempted to blow up the C&K tracks; in fact, Foxx wasn't yet sure which of the two had been responsible. Putting one brother in the pen would only deepen the hatred of the Becker clan. After his experience when trying to question Eddie, Foxx knew quite well that neither of the others could be forced or tricked into confessing.

"There's not any way to make beef stew till you've got the beef in the pot," he said, looking at the horse to avoid talking to himself. It was a habit he didn't like. He'd seen too many old solitaries walking along city streets with their lips working while they indulged in a solo conversation. "Looks like going on to the Becker place is my best bet. There'll be plenty of time to catch up with the brothers on the trail or after they get to Elko."

Foxx swung back into the saddle. The horse herd was in the distance now; small risk that any of the Beckers would look back and see him. He rode to the butte and backtracked on the wide swath of hoof-pocked earth, a ready-made path to his destination. As he rode Foxx wondered what the Becker womenfolk would be like, given the character of the brothers. At the end of another hour or more of steady riding, he had a chance to find out.

Foxx had been glancing at the declining sun occasionally as he rode and had noticed the gathering blackness at the horizon's rim. As the sun dropped lower, its face turned from the bright glare of molten brass to a ruddy pink that dyed the sky on both sides of it with purple-red streaks, and the black line of clouds rose to meet it. The sunset was a forewarning of one of the sudden summer storms that swept in quickly, with gusts of howling wind that turned the heavy rains the clouds dropped into leaden bullets. Foxx began to see a change at the same time that he saw the ranch house that snuggled against the upslope of the creek's shallow valley.

It was a low-roofed structure, part dugout, part stone. The stone was the tan brittle sandstone native to the area. Nevada settlers had quickly learned that the sandstone had formed in layers an inch to two inches thick. They'd discovered also that it was easy to split a layer away from those below it and to chip the sheets of porous rock into rectangles that could be laid flat between courses of adobe mortar. The walls of the Becker house extended from the bank, the roof below the creek valley's rim there, and little higher than a tall man's head in front. At one side of the house, only a few yards distant, a barn had been built of roughhewn boards. Between the barn and the creek there was a pole corral, a spring wagon standing beside it.

Foxx had gotten within fifty yards of the house when its roughhewn timber door swung open and a tall rectangular woman wearing a long calico dress stepped out. She cradled a double-barreled shotgun in her elbow in the manner of one accustomed to using it.

"Pull up where you are, mister!" she called. Her voice could have grated nutmegs.

Foxx reined in. "It's all right, lady. I don't mean to harm anybody." He was sure he was getting his first look at Ma Becker."

"That's what you say. What's your business here?"

Before Foxx could reply, a low rumble of distant thunder rolled across the sky. He turned in the saddle to look. The black cloud was high above the horizon now, ready to swallow the setting sun. Foxx jerked a thumb over his shoulder at the cloud.

"I saw the storm coming in. There's rain in those clouds, and I don't relish the idea of getting soaked."

"Too bad. You might not like it, but you better get used to it. We don't take in any Tom, Dick, or Harry that comes to our door."

"Your menfolks might not feel that way. Maybe if I could talk to your husband—"

"Menfolks are busy. Do what I say, now. Get on with you."

Another roll of thunder, heavier than the first, rippled over their heads. Foxx and the woman looked at the sky at almost the same time. The ominous black cloudline was stealing across the sun's face. The sky above the cloud was no longer rosy, but an unhappy blue. While Foxx and Ma Becker were still gazing at the sky a second woman came out.

That'd be Rose Becker, Foxx thought.

Rose was a younger version of her mother, just as angular, though not quite as tall. A stubby Whitneyville pocket pistol dangled from her hand.

"Ma, why don't you let him shelter?" Rose asked. She pointed to the threatening sky. "It's going to storm, and there ain't no use him getting soaked."

"Get back indoors, Rose!" Ma Becker snapped. "And this time, you stay there, like I told you to!"

More thunder sounded, louder now. Foxx added his voice to Rose's. "I said right off, lady, I didn't come here to harm anybody. If you'd see your way to letting me stay the night, and maybe feed me a bite of supper, I can pay."

Apparently Foxx had said the magic word. Ma Becker's face relaxed a little, but she still kept her eyes slitted suspiciously. Finally she said, "Well. A dollar for supper and breakfast and letting you sleep in the barn."

Foxx didn't want to appear too eager. He hesitated a moment before he agreed. "You made a bargain, lady." He dug a cartwheel out of his pocket and started to dismount, but Ma Becker swung the shotgun to ready.

"You don't get to come in the house. That ain't in the bargain. Toss me the money, then ride on over to the barn. You can put your animal inside, and I'll throw in what he'll eat. I'll bring your meal in a little while. But if you come skulking around the house, look out, mister! I'll be keeping this handy." She patted the shotgun's battered stock.

Foxx hurried to agree. "Whatever you say, ma'am. And I'm right obliged to you for keeping me dry tonight."

Ma Becker and Rose stood watching him as Foxx kneed the claybank over to the barn and swung to the ground. He led the animal inside. The barn was sturdier than it had looked. A low half-loft ran along one side; a row of chicken coops stood beneath it. Sacks of grain leaned on the back wall. On the other side there was room for a half-dozen stalls. There were horses in two of them.

Foxx busied himself taking the saddle off the gelding and hanging his rifle in its scabbard on one of several nails that had been driven into a post supporting the ridgepole; a lantern hung on one of the nails, harness straps on another. Foxx took the claybank's headstall from the saddle string that carried it, put it on the horse, and led the horse into one of the empty stalls. There was hay enough in the manger and water in a wooden bucket in one corner to see the horse through the night.

Walking back to the barn's long, clear center span, Foxx sat down beside his saddle and leaned back against its leather pommel. He took a stogie from his pocket and lighted it, dug out the bottle of whiskey from its wrappings, and treated himself to a generous swallow. Outside, darkness was arriving fast. Foxx got up long enough to light the lantern as lightning flared outside, thunder rolled, and the first spatters of rain tapped on the roof.

He'd smoked the stubby little twisted cigar almost

to its butt when Ma Becker hurried into the barn. She'd thrown a slicker over her head, and she carried a covered bowl. The sagging pocket of her apron suggested to Foxx that she was also carrying the short-barrelled Whitneyville pistol that Rose had been flourishing earlier.

"Here's your supper," Ma said ungraciously, thrusting the bowl into Foxx's hands. She noticed the cigar in his mouth. "Now, I won't have you setting my barn on fire with your dirty weed!" she snapped. "Put that thing out, and don't let me catch you lighting another one while you're here!"

Foxx dropped the cigar butt on the floor and ground it into the hard-packed earth with his bootheel. "Whatever you say, ma'am. But I've smoked cigars in a lot of barns before now and never have set one afire."

"There's always a first time," she retorted, turning to go. Over her shoulder, she told Foxx, "Don't bother to bring the dish back. I don't want you coming to my house. You remember that, and we won't have any trouble."

"Trouble's the last thing I want, ma'am," Foxx assured her. "And I thank you for my meal."

"You be ready to ride on as soon as you eat in the morning," she warned him. "And if you ever ride this way again, just go on past my place, because it won't do you no good to stop."

She flounced off, and Foxx sat down again. He removed the plate that covered the deep bowl. The bowl held two chicken legs and a wing, and a heap of white grainy hominy grits resting in a puddle of pale flour gravy. A battered teaspoon lay across the chicken pieces. Foxx looked at the food and shrugged. He hadn't really expected much better, and hot fried chicken beat cold jerky shavings and parched corn. Picking up one of the chicken legs, he began to eat.

Before Foxx had finished his supper, the rainstorm had grown in intensity. The noise of the drops spatting on the barn roof was an incessant tattoo reverberating in Foxx's ears. Now and then a sheet of lightning showed him the streaming ground outside the door illuminated in an instant of searing white brilliance, and the roll of thunder that always followed seemed to shake the earth. Two or three tiny leaks began in the roof, their drops catching the yellow glow of the lantern like miniature comets as they fell to the floor.

Foxx lighted an afterdinner stogie, in spite of Ma Becker's warning. He was reasonably sure that neither she nor Rose would leave the house as long as the rainstorm raged. Stretching his legs out on the packed earth in front of him, Foxx dug the bourbon bottle out of the saddlebag and lounged at ease while he sipped and puffed. He finished his cigar and stubbed out the butt. The wind had shifted, and an occasional chilling draft swept in through the doorless opening in the end of the barn. Though Foxx wasn't especially sleepy, there was nothing to do, and he concluded that he might just as well make up his bed.

Untying the saddle strings that secured his tarpaulin-wrapped blanket, Foxx threw the cylinder of bedding over one shoulder, took the lantern, and climbed the short slat ladder that led to the loft. The loft extended over half the length of the barn and stood just high enough above the wooden floor to allow a man to stand beneath it. Foxx looked around for loose hay to put under his blanket, but there was none. He held up the lantern. It showed a low stack of hay bales in the darkness at the loft's far end. Plenty of hay for a hundred beds, Foxx thought.

Foxx dropped the bedroll and walked over to the stack. He put the lantern down and began pulling hay out of the end of the top bale. The bale was tight, and Foxx heaved it down to the floor so he could get at the packed hay more easily. When he straightened up, he glanced idly at the stacked bales. Removing the bale that lay on the floor had bared a cavity in the bale below it. Foxx saw that the bottom bale was actually the butt end of a bale; the hay in the center had been cut out.

Picking up the lantern, Foxx raised it above his head. Inside the cavity, the light showed a sturdy wooden box. Foxx had seen enough such boxes that he didn't need the stenciled red words on its lid to tell him what was inside it. The words read: DANGER! DYNAMITE

Foxx moved over to the stacked hay and leaned down for a closer look. A coil of fuse lay beside the crate of explosive. He tried the lid experimentally; it came up in his hand. A round metal box lay in a vacant place where some of the dynamite sticks had been removed. It was labeled, too, and Foxx recognized the box by its shape and by the bright red stripes across its cover.

Very gingerly, he took out the container and twisted off its lid. Nestled in sawdust to keep them from exploding if they scraped along the interior of the box, the copper ends of blasting caps glinted in the lantern's rays. Foxx closed the box and set it carefully on the hay before returning to his inspection of the dynamite.

Almost all the sticks in the top layer had been removed from the wooden crate. Foxx was sure that he knew where four of those sticks were; they were in the drawer of his desk in the C&K's San Francisco office. He took two of the sticks from the box and brushed off the sawdust that clung to the greasy-slick casing. Rotating one of the sticks, he saw the name of the manufacturer embossed on the thick red cardboard tube. It was the same brand that had been used in the attempt to blow up the trestle.

Laying the dynamite aside, Foxx took the coil of

fuse out of the straw cavity and held it close to the lantern. The fuse was made by filling a woven linen tube with gunpowder-impregnated wax. Interlaced on the surface of the linen was a continuing spiral made of three strands of red threads. This, too, was the same marking that appeared on the lengths of fuse he'd taken from the explosives on the trestle.

Foxx fished out his pocketknife and cut off a foot-long piece of the fuse. He put the coil back with the box and replaced the blasting caps where he'd found them. He had no intention of taking the risk involved in carrying the unpredictable caps in his saddlebags. Then he put the lid back on the crate and returned the bale of hay to its original position, hiding the explosive cache.

Foxx picked up the two sticks of dynamite and the fuse and gazed at them for a moment. He nodded slowly, a nod of quiet satisfaction. He wasn't quite sure whether accident or instinct or deduction had led him to the hiding place of the dynamite. What had led him there wasn't important. Now he had what he'd been lacking; hard evidence—evidence that would stand up in court, evidence that would connect the Beckers with the effort to dynamite the C&K tracks.

All that remained for him to do was to get the evidence and the Becker brothers back to San Francisco and to stay alive himself in order to testify against them.

CHAPTER 12

Foxx picked up the lantern and clambered down the ladder. He took the bottle of bourbon out of his saddlebag and unwrapped it, then used the underwear to swathe the piece of fuse and the sticks of dynamite into a shapeless bundle. Carrying the dynamite that way didn't bother Foxx; he'd been around explosives enough to learn that fresh dynamite can be detonated only by a fuse or cap. He straightened up, the whiskey bottle in his hand, and lighted a stogie before taking a swallow of bourbon. The rain was still pelting down hard, but the wind had subsided. The worst of the sudden storm had passed.

Foxx walked to the barn door; while his bladder drained, he looked out into the black featureless void that the night had become. The windows of the house were dark. He took a final swallow of the whiskey and a last puff of the stogie before throwing the butt outside, where its glowing end quickly disappeared on the sodden ground. He put the uncushioned whiskey bottle in his saddlebag; if it got broken, that would be a small matter. The important thing was to hide and protect the evidence.

Before climbing back up to the loft, Foxx emptied

the mangers of the empty stalls and tossed the hay up
to the loft floor. He didn't want to disturb the stacked
hay bales any more than he had already. Up in the
loft again, he folded the tarpaulin and stuffed it with
the loose hay to make a thin mattress. He spread the
blanket out, unbuckled his gunbelt, and laid it near
the top of his bed. Sitting down, he slipped off his
boots and arranged them under the end of the blanket for a pillow before blowing out the lantern.
Crawling between the blanket's folds, he clasped his
hands behind his head and lay looking up into the
darkness.

He was still shifting around, trying to find the most
comfortable spot on the thin layer of hay between
him and the hard boards when the soft shuffling of
footsteps on the hardpacked dirt of the barn floor
reached his ears. Foxx tossed the blanket aside and
sat up. Sole leather grated on the ladder rungs. He
turned to reach for his gunbelt, but stopped when a
woman's voice spoke in a harsh whisper.

"Just stay still, mister. I got real good ears. I can
hear you moving around, and I'm aiming at the
noise. You pick up your pistol, and you'll be dead before you can shoot it."

Foxx never made the mistake of ignoring a threat
of that kind. He'd seen too many bodies of men shot
in the dark. He stopped, even though his position was
uncomfortable, propped up on his left arm, his right
reaching across his chest.

"That's good," the woman said. "You stay that way
till I tell you to move."

Though Foxx had been straining his ears as well as
his eyes, he couldn't tell whether the speaker was Ma
Becker or Rose. He recalled that their voices were
very much alike, and the whisper in which his visitor
spoke made it even more difficult for him to decide.
He stared in the direction from which the voice was
coming; the darkness of the night outside the doorless

opening was a shade brighter, but all that Foxx could see against it was a blurred outline.

He asked, "What's the trouble?"

"There's not no trouble. There won't be unless you're the one that makes it," she replied in the same strained whisper. He felt the cold steel of a pistol muzzle touch his cheek as the woman leaned over him. She cautioned him, "You just stay real still, now, and you won't get hurt a bit."

Foxx obeyed. The cold muzzle of the weapon left his cheek. A hand groped along his waist, found his belt, and pulled the buckle open. He felt knuckles dig into his abdomen as the buttons of his fly were unfastened. Then rough-workened fingers touched his flesh. They explored him, pushing his singlet open, and began feeling, hefting, squeezing.

"You sure ain't got very much down there," the woman whispered. Foxx could smell the stale sweatiness of her body as she leaned closer to him. Her hand left his crotch and pushed against his chest. "But I'll fix that, I bet. You lay back and stay still, now."

Again the pistol touched Foxx's face, and he lowered his shoulders to the blanket. Carefully, he folded his arms across his chest.

"Like this?" he asked.

"That's just fine. Now, don't move and make me shoot you."

After Foxx had lain quietly for a moment the gun's cold muzzle was taken from his face. He felt the hand slide back down his belly, and the fingers resumed their rough, unskilled caresses. In spite of himself, he felt an erection beginning.

"Now, that feels better," the woman breathed. "Just stay like you are and enjoy it the way I aim to."

Exploring and stroking became a tugging as the fingers closed around him. Foxx knew he was growing firmer but could not will himself to subside.

"You're feeling better to me all the time," the strange voice said. "Now don't you try to sit up and grab at me. I won't get so het up that I can't shoot if you do that."

Her threat was no idle one; Foxx understood that. The woman's hand was tugging at him more urgently now in response to his continued swelling. There was a swishing of cloth, and he caught a shadow of movement against the oblong of the doorway. Then she was kneeling over him, a leg on either side of his hips, pulling him up and arching her back to rub against his tip. Her breath was coming faster, and Foxx could feel the quivering of her thigh muscles where her straddling legs touched his sides. In one sudden motion she pulled her hand away and lowered herself on him, her thighs spreading away from him as he penetrated her.

Foxx was enclosed in warmth as her self-impalement continued until he was buried fully in her. She grunted with animal satisfaction. The grunt was followed by a series of deep sighs as she ground her pelvis down hard. Then she began back and forth above him, her knees thumping on the floor each time she brought her hips forward.

It would have been impossible for Foxx to have ignored her hot inner wetness, but even awareness did nothing for him. He lay still, staring hard, trying to discover which of the Becker women had mounted him, but all he could see was the suggestion of a head in outline, bobbing against the lighter darkness of the door opening. He told himself that it didn't matter which of the two women had decided to use him. Better being used than risking a panic shot that might kill him. He made no effort to respond to her movements but lay motionless, listening to her rasping breathing.

She was panting now, and Foxx could feel an urgent trembling begin in the tendons below her crotch, where they pressed into his hips. The urgency of her rocking increased. She bore down on him harder, her hips twisting, trying to force him deeper into her. Her pelvic bone was rubbing harder on his matted pubic hair, wet from the moisture she was releasing. She began to gasp. The gasps mounted quickly to a crescendo that became a single gutteral whistling inhalation. Her hip movements slowed and then stopped. She exhaled deeply and suddenly pulled away from him, leaving Foxx still erect and still unmoved.

"Now, you be smart and forget that anything ever happened," the woman whispered over the soft susurrus of clothing being rearranged. "As long as nobody don't know, there won't be nothing happen."

Foxx did not reply. She stood waiting for a moment, then he heard the small noises of her shoes scraping on the rungs of the ladder. He sat up and strained his eyes at the door opening, but all that he saw was the sudden dimming of its center by a shadow as the woman left. He still did not know whether his visitor had been Ma Becker or Rose.

Foxx pulled a stogie out of his shirt pocket and lighted it. His erection was subsiding and his crotch felt unpleasantly moist and sticky. Taking his bandana from his hip pocket he wiped himself dry and tossed the bandana aside. He felt that he needed a drink, but the thought of having to pull on his boots and go down the ladder to get the bourbon bottle robbed the idea of its appeal. He stood up, the moisture-saturated air surrounding him and hastening his fingers as he rearranged his clothing. The boards of the loft were cold under his feet. Foxx stubbed out the cigar and crawled back between the blankets. As soon as his feet warmed up, he went to sleep.

A rooster crowing in one of the coops under the loft roused Foxx. A minute might have passed, or ten, or an hour. Or the entire night, Foxx thought, looking at the barn door opening. The rain had stopped falling and the opening was brighter as the predawn gray took over the sky. The interior of the barn was cold, the moisture-saturated air clammy. The stamping of the horses in their stalls seemed to indicate that they, too, felt the effects of the wet atmosphere. Foxx pushed his feet out of the tousled bed and stood up. The boards of the loft were even colder than they'd been the night before, and he hurried to get his boots out and push his feet into them.

After he'd climbed down from the drafty loft, the barn's dirt floor seemed soft and warm. Foxx dug out the bourbon bottle and took a swallow. Only then did he light his first stogie, while he walked to the back of the barn to ease the night's pressure on his bladder. He looked around for a bucket of water, but except for those in the stalls, there were none. With a shrug, Foxx started for the creek that lay just beyond the corner of the corral.

There was no light showing in the window of the Becker house when Foxx left the barn, but when he returned, refreshed and wide awake in the fast-brightening gray, the window was glowing with yellow lamplight. The air was still crisp, and Foxx went back into the barn. He was standing with his back to the door, looking down at his saddle and wondering if the wisest thing for him to do might not be to ride on off without waiting for the breakfast he'd been promised, when a voice at the door broke the morning's stillness.

"Ma's fixin' breakfast." When Foxx turned to face her, Rose went on, "She sent me to see was you up, and to rouse you if you wasn't. I'll go tell her."

Foxx was studying the tall, angular girl, trying to satisfy his curiosity, and her words were slow to register. He finally replied. "Tell your ma I'll be riding out as soon as I eat."

Rose managed a stiff smile. "She said I was to tell you that; for you to get ready and be off our place as fast as you can."

Foxx nodded silently. He was still wondering, watching Rose's face for some indication of memory of guilt or pleasure, trying to catch some remembered inflection in her voice. Before he could reply, Rose turned and left.

Methodically and without haste, Foxx went to the loft and collected his gear. He buckled on his gunbelt and shook off the strands of loose hay the blanket had picked up before spreading it on the floor to fold and roll. The loft was darker than the floor below, and he stopped long enough to light the lantern. The blanket rolled and wrapped in the tarpaulin, he climbed back to the floor and hung the lighted lantern on its usual nail on the ridgepole post.

Before leading his horse out of the stall, Foxx laid out his gear in the order he'd need it: bit and bridle, saddle blanket and saddle, saddlebags, rifle in its stiff leather scabbard, and at the end of the neat row, the bedroll. Rose returned before he could carry his preparations further. She carried a tin plate; Foxx glanced at it. The grits of the morning were fried in brown crusted cakes. Two fried eggs lay beside them. The battered spoon on the plate looked like the one he'd used at supper.

She handed Foxx the plate and said, "Ma says not to bother to bring this to the house. And she says not to bother telling her good-bye."

"Fine. You can tell her I'll be as glad to go as she will to see me leave," Foxx replied matter-of-factly. He looked at the plate. A thin white line of grease was congealing around the eggs and grits-cakes. "I'll finish saddling as fast as I can, but I'm going to eat before these eggs get cold."

He sat down on the saddle. Rose was staring at the neat row in which he'd placed his gear. Foxx was eating hurriedly; his only idea was to get away from the Becker ranch as quickly as possible with the evidence in his saddlebags. He heard Rose inhale gustily and looked up from the plate just in time to see her running through the barn door.

Foxx stared as she disappeared. Her actions had been strange, but he'd come to expect strange behavior from the Beckers. He finished the eggs and scooped up the remaining grits, pushing them around the plate to mop up the last smears of the egg yolks. Putting the plate where he wouldn't step on it accidentally, he led the claybank out of the stall without taking time to light an after-breakfast stogie or take a second swallow of bourbon.

He bridled the gelding and slung the saddle on its back, cinched the girth, and threw the saddlebags over the pommel. Foxx was on tiptoe, leaning across the gelding's rump to reach the saddle strings that secured the bags when the almost noiseless whisper of footsteps brought him whirling around, reaching for his gun butt. He'd moved too late. Ma Becker was standing in the barn door, her shotgun not cradled in her elbow now but pointed directly at Foxx's chest.

"Take it easy, now," he urged. "I'm not moving."

"No, and you better not!" Ma Becker said grimly. Without turning her head, she commanded, "Rose!" Rose appeared behind her mother; she'd apparently been standing away from the door. Ma Becker said, "All right, Rose. Show me what you seen."

"It's on his rifle scabbard, Ma. Plain as daylight." Rose came into the barn, Ma Becker walking beside her, keeping the shotgun aimed at Foxx. Rose stopped beside what remained of the row of saddle gear and pointed to the scabbard. "There. Branded on, just like I told you."

Foxx dropped his eyes involuntarily to see what Rose was pointing out and cursed himself for a careless fool. He'd become so used to the practice of railroads in labeling even the smallest item of their property that it hadn't occurred to him to inspect the rifle scabbard on both sides. There it was, staring at him, branded indelibly into the leather just as Rose had said: C&K RR.

When Foxx raised his eyes they met Ma Becker's accusing glare. "So that's why you come snoopin' around here! Lookin' for my boys, I'll bet! Fixin' to get even with 'em!"

"Get even for what?" Foxx asked. If he needed any confirmation after finding the dynamite cache that one of the Becker brothers had made the effort to blow up the Solano County trestle, he'd just gotten it.

Ma Becker ignored his question. She said, "That damned C&K killed my baby! Now you're out to get my other boys just because they keep on plaguing you to own up it was your fault my Freddie died!"

"Nobody's after your sons for anything they didn't do," Foxx said.

"See, Ma!" Rose broke in. "He's owning up that he works for the railroad! I told you, didn't I?"

"Hush up, girl! I'm trying to think what to do!" her mother commanded.

Foxx decided he had nothing to lose. "There's not much you can do with me, old woman. Not unless you trigger that shotgun. And if you do that, woman or not, you'll hang for it."

"Oh, I don't guess I would! Who'd know about it? Folks just drop out of sight in this desert country. Nobody ever finds out what happened to 'em."

There was enough truth in what she said to make Foxx think hard. "That's not going to happen to me. My men in Elko know where I was heading. If I don't show up there by tomorrow, they'll be coming here to look for me."

"You're lying!" she snapped. "Just like all you railroaders!"

"You'll be real sorry if you don't listen to me," Foxx warned her.

"Shut up!" she ordered. "I'm still trying to think!"

"Maybe he's not lying, Ma," Rose suggested. "If I was you—"

"Well, you ain't! And shut up, like I told you to!"

Rose fell silent. She looked at her mother, a worried frown wrinkling her forehead. Foxx looked at the Becker matriarch, too, but he kept his face placidly immobile.

"All right!" Ma Becker finally announced. "I figured out what we've got to do. Rose, you throw a saddle on the gray. You know where the boys are. Chase after 'em and tell 'em to hyper back here as fast as they can ride!"

"Ma," Rose protested, "the boys left here yesterday. I never would catch up to 'em!"

"Yes, you will! You know how slow they got to move when they're drivin' a herd. They wasn't planning on going past Pine Canyon last night, and they won't be starting outa there until about now. You do what I tell you, girl! Get moving!"

"What about him?" Rose asked, indicating Foxx.

"Don't fret over him. I'll keep this scattergun on his belly until you get back. You and the boys oughta be here a little while after dark. Now, get on with it, girl!"

Rose started to argue further, but the glare on her mother's face made her close her mouth without speaking. She led a gray pony out of its stall and threw a saddle over its back. In less than five minutes she had mounted and was on her way.

Ma Becker told Foxx, "Now, then. Throw that pistol down on the ground in front of me, where I can get to it easy." Foxx made no move to obey her. She repeated, "You heard what I said! I want that gun of yours!"

"Then, come after it," Foxx invited her. He kept his voice low and calm.

"Hah! And get near enough so you can make a grab for my shotgun! Not much I won't! You don't fool me for a minute, you dirty railroading bastard!"

"Shoot me, then," Foxx invited. He looked at her, his face expressionless.

Foxx was gambling, but it was a gamble he planned to win. He didn't want to shoot Ma Becker, but it wasn't in his plans for her to shoot him, either. When she'd moved into the circle of light cast by the lantern, he'd noticed something that he hadn't been able to see while she was standing against the dim dawnlight in the doorway.

Ma Becker's weapon was an ancient Poultney hammerlock, and neither of its hammers had been cocked. As long as Rose had been present, Foxx had to consider the possibility that she might be carrying the Whitneyville pistol she'd been holding the evening before, and that would have made the odds too long.

He watched her impassively as she raised the shotgun to her shoulder and her finger sought the trigger. For a moment, Foxx thought he'd miscalculated. He gauged the distance between them. He saw Ma Becker's finger tighten on the trigger and jumped forward as she tried to fire the gun. When it failed to go off, Foxx got a glimpse of the consternation on her face, and as he was closing in on her, reaching for the shotgun barrel, she managed to bring her thumb up and pull one of the hammer's back.

Foxx had his hand on the shotgun's barrel by that time, and was forcing the muzzle up, over his head. He pulled at the barrel, trying to take the weapon away from her, and the trigger she'd cocked fell. Simultaneously, the shotgun blasted its load of pellets into the roof of the barn, the barrel twisted in Foxx's hand, and the force of the discharge sent the stock of the loosely held weapon flying into Ma Becker's jaw.

She was knocked senseless by the blow. Without a
sound, she crumpled to the ground.

Dropping the shotgun, Foxx bent over the old
woman's prone form. He felt the pulse fluttering in
her thin corded throat, saw no blood on her face or
body, and concluded that she'd simply been knocked
out.

He wasted no time after that. Stopping only long
enough to slide his rifle into the scabbard and secure it
with quick knots tied in the saddle strings, Foxx
swung up on the horse. Ducking low to clear the top
of the barn door, he set off in pursuit of Rose.

CHAPTER 13

Although the day had begun, the sun had not yet come up. The sky was completely clear, no clouds hung above the earth to catch the first rays of the sun, so there was not a tinge of pink overhead when Foxx emerged from the barn. Rose had ridden up the slope of the creek valley and disappeared over its crest, but the prints of her mount were pressed deep into the rain-softened soil. Puddles filled every depression, the water they held shining like freshly melted lead, reflecting the hue of the sky.

Foxx kept the claybank at a lope as he rode up the long rise that led to level but broken ground. The horse broke gait more than once when its hooves slipped in the water-softened earth, but recovered quickly and forged ahead. At the top of the slope, Foxx followed the hoofmarks with his eyes until he glimpsed Rose. She held a good lead on him, perhaps two miles, Foxx judged. He dug his heels into the gelding's flanks, and the rawboned animal responded with a bit more speed.

Rose vanished around the end of a low butte. Foxx did not try to increase the gelding's speed. Yesterday, when he'd crossed the path of her brothers and the horse herd they were driving, he'd been ten or a dozen miles from the Becker's ranch. The herd could not have gone more than three or four miles further, and it was just getting started by now. At best, Rose could not catch up with them until noon, or early afternoon. Mustang herds could not be hurried, or the skittish animals would bolt and scatter. Foxx could foresee a long day ahead of him, and a long day with an overtired horse made a bad combination.

Before Foxx reached the butte where Rose had disappeared, the sun came up. Its rays warmed Foxx's back as he rounded the end of the rock outcrop from which erosion had formed the butte. Rose still had not seen him. She was pushing steadily ahead, never turning to see what lay behind her.

Knows exactly where the Becker boys were headed for—Pine Valley, the old woman said it was, Foxx thought.

For several miles ahead, the land was relatively level. Foxx reined in to rest his horse, though the gelding was holding its gait well. He took advantage of the pause by lighting up a stogie. Through the pungent blue smoke that wreathed his head in the windless morning air, he kept his eyes fixed on Rose. When he judged the claybank had rested long enough, Foxx took up his pursuit again.

He'd been riding not more than five minutes when he saw that Rose was doing what he'd just done, stopping to give her mount a breather. For the first time since Foxx had been following her, she looked back. Even if Foxx had been forewarned, there would have been no place for him to hide. The high mesaland at that point was as flat and featureless as a prairie. Foxx kept forging steadily ahead, but Rose took off at a gallop.

Thankful that he'd halted when he did and that the claybank would be fresher than the gray Rose was on, Foxx followed Rose's move. He pushed the geld-

ing to a gallop. On the horizon he could see the jut-
ting humps that indicated they were approaching
broken country again. It was terrain that Rose knew
and Foxx did not. Given the advantage of rough terrain, scored by valleys and marked by small mesas
and buttes, the advantage that Foxx had enjoyed until now would be lost.

Slowly, the claybank pulled up on the gray. Foxx
could feel his mount straining from time to time, and
sacrificed some of the distance he gained by reining
in for a few moments and letting the claybank walk.
Rose's horse was beginning to tire. Its head was
drooping, and its gait growing ragged, but Rose did
not allow the animal to slow its pace. Foxx was gaining ground steadily now as the gray became more and
more exhausted. Its legs were no longer moving in
smooth rhythm, and it broke stride occasionally as it
splashed through the puddles that last night's rain
had left standing in hollows.

Rose was looking behind often now as Foxx closed
the distance between them. He was gaining faster as
the gray's stamina faltered more and more. The gap
between the two riders narrowed from the two miles
it had been earlier to a mile, then a half mile, and
still Foxx continued to pull closer. When he'd narrowed the space to a hundred yards or so, Foxx saw
Rose groping in the pocket of the apron she'd not
had time to take off before leaving the Becker barn.
She twisted in the saddle, and Foxx saw the sunlight
glinting on the nickel plate of the little Whitneyville
pocket pistol that Rose had been carrying the night
before.

Foxx did not slacken speed. He knew the range of
the small .31 caliber revolver was not great enough
for one of its slugs to reach him. A spurt of smoke
came from the pistol's muzzle as Rose fired. Foxx did
not see where the bullet hit the wet ground. She trig-
gered the little pistol again and yet again. Foxx could

not hear the spatting report of the Whitneyville; he counted Rose's shots by the muzzle blast. He kept the claybank at a gallop, though it, too, was beginning to tire.

Rose shot twice in quick succession as she saw Foxx overtaking her so rapidly. Then disaster struck her. The gray had been running almost wildly while she was trying to bring Foxx down with her weapon. Its hooves splashed into a wide puddle, slid in the soft mud of its bottom. With an ungainly thrashing of its weakening legs, the horse fought to keep erect. Rose's arms were flailing in the air. Foxx saw the bright arc the pistol made as it sailed from her hand and fell to the ground. The gray was sliding in fetlock-deep water, thrashing in panic as its hooves found no traction in the soft mud.

Rose could keep her balance no longer. She toppled from the saddle. The sudden loss of its rider threw the horse out of balance. It staggered and skidded and went down with a splash that drenched Rose and sent a sheet of spray shooting up to shimmer diamondlike in the bright morning sun.

Foxx reined the gelding out of its gallop and down to an easy lope. By the time he pulled up beside Rose, the horse's panting had eased. Foxx dismounted and walked over to where Rose was lying at the edge of the subsiding puddle. The gray had regained its feet and stood a few paces away, its legs trembling and its sides heaving.

Seeing Foxx approaching, Rose tried to stand up. One of her legs buckled when she raised herself from the ground, and she would have fallen if Foxx had not caught her. She struggled to get away from him. Foxx released her and stepped back and she crumpled to the ground again.

"My leg," she said, bewilderment in her voice. "I think my leg's broke."

"Wouldn't surprise me a bit," Foxx told her. He took a step forward. "Here. I'll give you a hand."

"Keep away from me!" she snarled. "Don't you dare to touch me!"

Foxx stepped back, took a stogie out of his shirt pocket, and lighted it. Rose sat at the puddle's edge, watching him. She did not try to move, and after he'd waited a few moments, Foxx said, "Well, go ahead. Get up."

"I—I can't," she confessed. "My leg don't work."

Foxx took his time replying. "Well, then, it seems to me like you've got two choices. You can sit in that mud and water till somebody comes along you'll let help you." He waved his cigar at the deserted landscape. "That might be a while, of course, and I'd bet you'd get mighty tired and hungry while you waited. Or, you can show some sense and let me help you."

She glared at Foxx for a long minute. He puffed his stogie and said nothing. Finally Rose asked him, "What will you do if I let you help me back on my horse?"

"You might just as well face it, Rose," Foxx told her, his voice coolly impersonal. "You won't be able to stay on that horse until your leg's fixed up."

She sat silent again, thinking over what he'd said. Pressing her lips into a hard, straight line, she grasped her leg with both hands and tried to bend it to place her foot on the ground. A grimace of pain broke the hard set of her face, and she gave up trying.

"You didn't tell me what I asked you," she said at last.

"About what I'll do?" When Rose nodded, Foxx went on, "I'd say a fair exchange might be for you to guide me wherever your brothers are. I've got no business with you, but I sure have with them."

"No!" Rose snapped. "You won't never make me do that! You want to put 'em in jail, don't think I don't know it! I'll set here till I rot afore I show you where they are!"

"I'll just have to find 'em myself, then," Foxx replied. "Or go into Elko and wait until they drive that horse herd they're wrangling into the stockpens. It won't be much of a trick for me to catch them."

Rose gazed at Foxx thoughtfully while she thought over what he'd said. The full meaning of his casual statement finally sank in. She asked him, "You mean to say you'd go on off after them and leave me here with my leg busted I don't know how bad?"

Foxx kept his voice cold. "If you make me do it that way. Or you can be sensible and take me wherever they are now. I'd say they can't be much past that place your ma said something about."

"Pine Canyon?"

Foxx nodded. "I can find it without you, you know. I've got a map that shows it."

"There's a lot of canyons around. You won't know whether you got the right one or not, even if you have got a map."

"Then I'll follow the map to where I think it is and circle until I cross their trail. That'll be easy, wet as the ground is."

Rose fell silent again. Foxx finished his stogie and lighted a fresh one. Finally she said reluctantly, "I guess maybe you're right. I'll show you where Pine Canyon is."

"I'll have to fix your leg up first. You can't ride unless it's got a splint of some kind to keep it from wobbling. It's going to hurt, too, but I'll be as gentle as I can."

Foxx looked around. The only growing thing that resembled wood was a clump of sagebrush a few dozen paces away. He took out his knife as he walked over to the low gray-green bushes and by cutting their bigger branches off close to the roots managed to get enough pieces long enough and stiff enough to serve as a temporary splint. Trimming and smoothing their rough bark as he walked, he went back to Rose.

"Here," he said, handing her the knife. "It's your leg. Cut some strips off the bottom of your dress so I'll have some bandages for it."

Rose scowled, and Foxx thought for a moment she was about to refuse. Then she took the knife and scored the hem of her ankle-length dress and tore off several strips.

Foxx bandaged the leg first, to reduce the swelling that was beginning and to keep the sagebrush twigs from chafing her skin. Then he bound the strips over the bandage. He asked Rose, "How does that feel?"

"I'll manage all right," she said curtly. "Just lead the horse over so I can get on."

She winced when Foxx helped her to her feet and assisted her as she clambered into the saddle. Once, as he was helping her to fit the broken leg into the stirrup, he had an impulse to ask her if she'd been the one who'd visited him in the loft, but the thought seemed foolish even as it occurred, and he stayed as silent as she did.

When Rose was settled in the saddle he asked her, "How does your leg feel now?"

"It hurts, as if you didn't know," she replied ungraciously. "But I'll manage all right."

Foxx had linked the gray's reins into a single long strap. It made a short lead rope, but he didn't want to encourage Rose to try to escape by letting her control her horse. He swung into the claybank's saddle and they moved off. Attending to the broken leg had eaten up time, and the sun was well above the horizon when they started.

"Which way?" he asked Rose. She pointed, and he reined the gelding over to follow the course she'd indicated.

Fast movement wasn't possible with the gray being led. Foxx chafed at their slow progress. At the rate

they were traveling, they'd do well to overtake the
Becker boys before they reached Elko. As they moved
over the trackless terrain, Foxx began to worry. The
entire landscape was strange to him. He hadn't seen
any of the landmarks he remembered having passed
on his way to the Becker ranch the day before: un-
usual rock formations, distinctive ridges, prominent
buttes. With the tracks of the horse herd obliterated
by the rain, he had only his map or Rose's directions
to go by.

Foxx scowled. He took the map out again and
studied it. He'd already looked for Pine Canyon on it,
but the topographer hadn't bother to note the
names of any features except the streams and the tal-
lest mountains. They'd crossed no streams since leaving the spot where Rose had fallen, and the only
mountain he could both see clearly and identify was
the rounded summit of Ruby Dome. Orienting the
direction Rose was guiding him with the dome, Foxx
suspected that they were too far south to be on a
course that would intercept the Becker brothers.

Foxx looked at the map again. Logic told him that
Rose was lying, instinct told him they were too far
south. The sun and his stomach told him it was
nearly noon. If Rose had been leading him in the
right direction, there should be fresh tracks, made after the rain, if they'd moved on after daybreak. The
combination of logic and instinct was too strong to ig-
nore.

"You sure we're going the right way, Rose?" he
asked.

"Now, that's a fool question for a grown man to
ask, even if he is a railroader."

"I think you're trying to trick me."

"Like you tricked me and Ma to taking you in last
night?" she retorted quickly. Then, to try to cover her
hasty words, she added, "If you don't like the way I'm

showing you to go, pick out some other direction yourself."

Folding the map, Foxx tucked it away. He nudged the claybank gelding's flank and turned its head northeast.

Rose called, "Wait a minute! You're going the wrong way!"

"No, I'm not. You just told me if I didn't like the way you've been taking us to pick out a direction of my own that I like better. That's what I'm doing."

Rose glared at him but said nothing. If Foxx had needed anything but his own deductions to tell him he was at last moving in the right direction, her sour scowl provided it.

As they moved on, the character of the terrain changed. The land over which they'd been traveling had been level and relatively smooth; now it began to slope downward in an easterly direction, into a wide shallow valley, dry and void of vegetation. Seams opened in the bare soil in a pattern of parallel gullies. Most of these were so narrow a man could step across them, but a few were too wide for a horse to leap. Foxx was forced to move in a series of zigzags as they traversed the erosion-slashed terrain.

For almost an hour they moved in a long slant along the slope, and eventually the slope leveled out. Foxx studied the map again, decided that they'd reached the valley's floor, and reined the gelding to follow the slow curve it made to the north. A dark spot showed in the distance. As they approached it, the spot grew larger and took on the form of a large shrub or stunted tree. Still closer, the dark hue seemed slowly to grow lighter and become green. When they were very close, Foxx could identify it as a pine tree, a poor example of its kind, but a pine tree just the same. Just behind it a crevasse that sliced into the slope became visible.

"That's Pine Canyon up ahead, isn't it?" he asked Rose.

Rose compressed her lips until they disappeared in a thin stubborn line, but said nothing. Foxx waited until he faced the front again before he began smiling with grim satisfaction. He said nothing more to Rose.

Foxx had noticed the first tracks at about the time he'd been able to identify the tree ahead of him as a pine. Signs of the night's rainstorm had almost disappeared. Between the thirsty soil and bright hot sun the puddles that had been so frequent at dawn had vanished, and the surface of the earth was nearly dry. While the storm that swept the high plateau had wiped the soil's surface clean of old tracks, it had formed a matrix for those made after the downpour passed.

There had been only a few hoofprints distant from the pine tree, but these had given Foxx his first clue as to what might, almost must, have happened. The tracks multiplied as they came closer to the tree. When they reached a point where Foxx could look into the crevasse that opened behind the pine, he saw that it was bigger than he'd expected it to be, a wide box canyon with steep walls gouged out by some whim of nature. Tethering the gelding to the pine and still ignoring Rose, Foxx walked into the canyon.

Now his Comanche training served him well once more. He saw the traces of a small fire, rain-scattered ash and bits of charred, half-burned wood. He squatted where the fire had been, pinched up a sampling of the ash, and smelled it as he rubbed it between his fingers. The fire had been fresh last night, not one that had been kindled days or weeks ago. He walked on into the canyon and began to cover it from wall to wall in a series of wide arcs.

He walked slowly, his eyes fixed on the ground,

reading the tracks as though they were words printed on a page.

By the time he'd covered the canyon floor and returned to the mouth, Foxx knew almost precisely what had happened during the night. Deep holes and clods of disturbed earth marked the points on each side of the opening where picket pins had been driven and lariats stretched across the gap to turn the canyon into a temporary corral for fifty or sixty mustangs. Sometime during the storm the thunder and lightning had started the horses milling; then they had panicked. Gouges higher than his head on the canyon walls told Foxx that some of the mustangs had tried to go up them and slid back.

Soon the mustangs had bolted through the canyon mouth. The three men riding shod horses had saddled and ridden after the mustangs; their running footprints were superimposed on the tracks left by the mustangs' unshod hooves. Foxx followed the tracks outside the canyon. On the valley floor the herd had ceased to be a herd; the half-wild ponies had scattered in small bunches, and the men on their shod horses had divided to trail them, each rider going in a different direction.

Foxx had been aware that Rose was watching his every move, but he said nothing when he returned to the tethered horses. She lacked the stubborn stamina of her brothers, or had more curiosity, for when Foxx still did not speak as they rode off she asked, "Where are you taking me now?"

"Elko."

"Why?"

"That horse herd your brothers drove panicked in the storm last night. The mustangs broke out and scattered. Your brothers are trying to round 'em up again now."

"How do you know?"

"Tracks," Foxx said laconically. Rose asked more

questions as they rode on toward Elko, but Foxx's stubborn streak had surfaced now. He paid no attention to Rose's questions but let all of them remain unanswered as they rode on toward Elko.

CHAPTER 14

When Foxx ignored her questions after he'd answered the first three, Rose fell silent. Foxx did not speak, either. He looked back at her only after they'd traversed a rough section of the high plateau's broken ground, to see how she was standing up. Invariably, she turned her head so their eyes would not meet, but no matter how rough the going, she did not complain.

On the first stage of the trip Foxx had maintained an easy pace to reduce the pain that her horse's uneven gait might cause Rose. Now he ignored the discomfort of her injured leg and pushed the horses hard.

Setting his course by the sun and his map, he rode in as straight a line as the rugged terrain allowed. He reined the claybank gelding up ridges and down canyon walls that earlier he would have detoured. The lead line between the claybank and the gray was never allowed to slacken. The only consideration he gave to the comfort of Rose or himself he showed when they reached the south bank of the Humboldt River. Foxx rode beside the rain-swollen stream until he found a shallow spot where the river could be forded instead of forcing the horses to swim.

At the C&K depot in Elko, Foxx tied the animals to the hitchrack behind the depot that was reserved for railroad employees. Rose still did not speak to him or question him. Foxx left her sitting in the grays' saddle, still glowering. He went up to Bob Scott's office.

"Foxx!" Scott didn't try to hide the relief in his voice. "You're back sooner than I expected you to be. Were you lucky or otherwise?"

"About half and half, Bob." Foxx settled into a chair, glad to be in a seat that didn't move. He reached in his pocket for a stogie, but the pocket was empty.

"You didn't catch up with the Beckers?"

"Not all of 'em. But I look for the three boys to blow into town real soon."

"By noon tomorrow. Before dark, for sure. So I'm in a hurry to get things ready before they get here."

"I never knew you when you weren't in a hurry," Scott grinned. "All right. What comes first?"

"I've got a woman downstairs who needs a doctor. And I want to put her someplace she can't just walk away from if she takes a mind to."

"Doc Shaler handles all the C&K cases here," Scott said. "He's got a spare room behind his office with a bed or two in it where he keeps our out-of-town cases. Who's the woman, Foxx?"

"Rose Becker."

Scott expelled his breath in a long whistle. "How'd you manage to bring in the Becker boys' sister without them shooting you full of holes? Or did you just shoot first?"

"It just happened they weren't around. And I didn't shoot anybody, but Ma Becker damn near ventilated me."

"How?"

"It'd take too long to go into now. I'll tell you later on."

"What about the brothers? Where were they when all this was going on?"

"They were on their way here, driving a horse herd. That storm last night spooked the mustangs and they lost their herd. They're out rounding it up now. I'd imagine they'll finish the job about dark and bring the mustangs in tomorrow. They don't even know yet that I'm around, much less that I plan to be on hand down at the pens to bid 'em welcome."

"A hot one, is my guess," Scott said.

"That'll depend on them, Bob." Foxx was speaking very soberly now. "Damn it, Bob, I don't want those three cut down in a shootout on C&K property. I want to put them behind bars after they've been tried in court. And in my saddlebags downstairs, I've got the evidence that'll convict them. I'm out to show everybody that you can't put dynamite on C&K tracks without paying for it."

Scott nodded thoughtfully, "I see what you're getting at. If there's a shootout and the Beckers get killed, there'll always be people who'll say the C&K hires killers to cut down innocent men without trials. Well, go ahead. What else do you need?"

"Enough men standing up with me when the Beckers get here so they can see from the start they wouldn't have a chance if they force a fight."

"Put it into numbers for me, Foxx."

Foxx rubbed his chin, noted absently that he could stand a shave, and finally said thoughtfully, "Flaherty's got two yard bulls stationed here. One at the division point in Carlin. The only man I've got close is Matt Grey at the division. That sure ought to be plenty."

"Wait a minute," Scott cautioned. "Flaherty's divi-

sion bull is up at the Bullion mine, guarding a
payroll shipment. He rode the regular Bullion freight
drag that pulled out an hour ago, and he won't be
back until late tomorrow night. One of the bulls from
the yard here's been out sick for two days. He might
be fit to look after the Becker woman by now,
though."

"Which leaves my division man and one yard bull
from here and me," Foxx thought aloud. He shook
his head. "That's not enough. If it's man for man, the
Beckers will come in shooting. I'd bet my life on that.
And I don't want shooting, damn it!"

"I don't imagine our bosses do, either." Scott hesitated for a moment. "I'll stand up with you, Foxx.
You know that."

"Sure. Thanks, I'll ask you to do just that. Now,
let's see. The Becker boys can't get that herd of
mustangs put together again in time to start for Elko
tonight. Noon tomorrow's the soonest they could get
here."

"Whatever you say, Foxx."

Foxx reached across Scott's desk for a pad of flim-
sies and pulled the inkstand closer. He picked up one
of the pens from the grooves at the base of the stand
and wrote rapidly in an open schoolboy script, then
passed the pad back to Scott. "This'll get my man up
from Carlin. There's a freight or work car or something he can take, I guess? He won't have to wait until the Flyer passes tomorrow?"

"There's a short night drag, empties. He can hop
it."

"Fine. I'll tell the hotel lady he'll need a room."

"He can sleep in one of the cabooses on a siding.
No use in going to all that trouble."

"No. I don't sleep in cabooses when I'm on a case,
Bob. I don't ask my men to, either."

"Suit yourself, Foxx. What about the other men
you'll need?"

"You know the crew here better than I do. Find me two men with the guts to stand their ground and who've got cool enough heads not to get spooked and start shooting unless I tell them to."

"Calkins and Barnes," Scott said promptly. "They're both veterans. Fought on different sides, of course, but there's no more hard feelings left between them."

"I'll take them on your say-so, Bob. Nine o'clock tomorrow morning. Get out enough of those Winchesters you've got so each man has one. I want the Beckers to see plenty of guns, right out in the open. Might keep 'em from being too quick to start something." Scott nodded, and Foxx went on, "If you'll have your clerk or somebody you can depend on get Rose Becker settled in at the doctor's place, and take that horse back to the stockpens, it'll save me some time. The doctor knows your men; I'd have to do a lot of explaining."

"I'll get somebody to take care of it," Scott replied. "And you'll have the men you need in the morning. Including me."

"Thanks, Bob." Foxx stood up and stretched. "I'm too damn soft, been sitting at a desk too long. I need a soak and a shave. And to catch up with my sleep. I'll be at the hotel if you need me for anything. If you don't, I'll see you in the morning."

With his Winchester in one hand and his saddlebags over his shoulder, Foxx reached the door of the Depot Hotel just as Joyce Kilpatrick came out. She stopped and looked at his rough clothes.

"Foxx! I didn't recognize you at first. You look like you've just come back from a hunting trip."

"I guess you could say that's what I've been doing. I sure hope your gear got here all right."

"It did, thanks to you. Cap's out at the Humboldt Hotel right now, getting everything ready for tomorrow. I hope you're going to be there?"

"What time's your big show going to be?"

"Four o'clock. The air's still warm close to the ground, and the wind's usually gentle, so I shouldn't drift too far."

"You mean you just go where the wind takes you?"

"Of course. Some kinds of balloons can be steered, but mine isn't one of them."

Foxx shook his head. "I still say I'll keep at least one foot on the ground."

"You might like it up there if you tried it. You get a wonderful view of everything. In country like this you can see for miles all around you, even without going very high. But come out and watch the ascension, at least."

"I sure will try to make it, Joyce. If I get my business in hand in time, you can count on it. I guess you're on your way to help get things fixed up?"

"Oh, no. It's an all-night job, and Cap insists on doing everything himself. He says that's the only way to be sure it's done the right way. So I'm going to eat supper and go to bed and rest. That's my way of getting ready for tomorrow."

Foxx looked at Joyce for a moment. She was wearing a dress of thin, soft-woven wool, a pale tan, that made her blond hair seem straw-light. He said, "If you're not too hungry to wait until I clean up and change my clothes, maybe you'll have supper with me."

"I'd like to," she said unhesitatingly. "And I'm not really that hungry. I just didn't have anything else to do, and I'm tired of sitting in a hotel room waiting for time to pass."

"I'll tap at your door as soon as I'm ready, then. And I'll hurry, so that you won't have to wait too long."

In his room, Foxx took the bourbon bottle out of his saddle bags and stowed the bags with the evidence he'd uncovered safely in the back of the closet. He swallowed a hasty sip of bourbon while he gathered fresh clothing, the clean singlet and shirt from his valise, his suit from the hanger, and his shaving gear. In the bathroom at the end of the hall he quickly got rid of the grime of two days in the saddle and the clinging aroma that he still carried from his encounter with Rose or Ma Becker—he'd still not figured out which of them it'd been—during his night in the barn. Just a bit more than a half hour later he tapped on Joyce Kilpatrick's door.

"Come in, Foxx," she called.

Foxx entered. Joyce was sitting on the bed. She'd changed from the wool dress into a robe of clinging chiffon. The bedside table, a duplicate of the one in the room Foxx occupied, had been moved from its place against the wall to the floor at one side of the bed. Plates covered with napkins were on the table. A bottle of wine, its cork already drawn, stood swathed in a napkin between the plates. Foxx's jaw dropped. He stood in the doorway staring at the table.

"Maybe you'd better come in and close the door," Joyce suggested. "I'm not sure Mrs. Fogarty would approve of us having dinner together in one of her rooms."

"My guess is that she wouldn't." Foxx closed the door and stepped closer to the table. "But it beats me how you ever got a meal served up here at all. I sure didn't think I was taking a lot of time changing."

"You took exactly the right amount of time. After we'd talked outside and you went in, I just happened to see the waiter from the station lunchroom carrying a tray back from that palace car that's waiting on the siding, the one that belongs to the Winona mine. I decided if they could serve a railroad car, they could serve us. So—" Jocye waved her hand over the table.

"It's a fine idea. Even wine."

"We'd better start now, or everything will be cold. If you'll pour the wine, Foxx—"

As they ate, Foxx said between bites, "Tell me what you're going to do tomorrow."

"That'd spoil your surprise tomorrow, when you see it!" Joyce protested.

"I might not be able to make it, Joyce, I'll try, of course."

"You haven't finished hunting, then? A criminal of some kind?"

"Two, maybe three of them."

"Bad men? Dangerous?"

"I suppose you'd call them that. If my plans works out, though, there won't be any trouble."

"By trouble, you mean shooting?" When Foxx nodded, she said, "And you think ballooning's risky! I'd much rather be up by myself in the nice peaceful sky than to be shooting and being shot at!"

"By yourself?" Foxx frowned. "I thought your manager or helper, this fellow Cap—I thought he goes up with you."

"Of course not! His job is to watch where the air currents take the balloon and follow it and pick me up when I land."

"Suppose you land too hard?"

Joyce shook her head. "There's not much danger of that. I just pour water on the burner, and when the balloon gets less hot air, it comes down slowly. If it starts falling too fast, I drop some ballast."

"It still sounds risky. I'll take my chances while my feet are on good, solid ground."

Joyce pushed her plate away and held out her wineglass. "We ought to have at least one afterdinner toast, Foxx."

Foxx poured for her and replenished his own glass. Joyce held up her wineglass.

"Success to our ventures," she said. "On the ground, in the air—or wherever they may lead us."

As she drank, Joyce looked at Foxx over the rim of her glass. The promise in her eyes was unmistakable. Foxx drained his glass and set it on the table. Joyce still held her wineglass to her lips. Foxx took it from her hand and put it beside his. He leaned across the table and she bent forward to meet him. Their lips met, hers still wet with wine. Foxx tasted the vintage as she parted her lips and invited his tongue, met it with the quivering tip of her own.

When they broke the kiss, Foxx asked, "Is this the kind of venture you had in mind?"

"What else? Can you think of a better one for two people who're so much alike and yet so different?"

Foxx stood up and moved the table away from the bed. Joyce caught his hand and placed it on her breast. Foxx felt her nipple, budded firm against his palm. He cupped it, squeezing gently, and Joyce shivered. She still had a hand on his wrist, and she pulled him down on the bed beside her. Foxx bent and nuzzled aside the loose collar of her robe, his lips moving as he swept them from her earlobes to the end of her shoulder. Her skin was warmly fragrant with a light but sensuous perfume. Foxx was coming erect now. He stood up and began to shed his coat.

Joyce sat on the bed, leaning back, her hands behind her, propping her up. One of her shoulders had been bared when Foxx pushed her robe aside to caress it; on that side the collar sagged almost to her waist to show the top of a small high-set breast and part of its delicate pink aureole. When Foxx had tossed his coat and vest aside and was unbuttoning his shirt, Joyce said, "Sit down, Foxx. I'll take off your boots."

He lay back on the bed and raised his legs. Joyce straddled one leg, grasped the heel of his boot, and levered it off. She slid the other boot off and tugged at his touser cuffs, dragging them off his legs. Foxx stood up, unfastening the buttons of his singlet. Joyce stood in front of him, her eyes on the bulge that had grown from his crotch. As Foxx shrugged his shoulders free to let his singlet fall, she dropped her arms and let her robe slide to the floor.

They stood facing one another, naked. Foxx gazed at Joyce's slim body. It was like that of a young girl just coming to maturity, scantily fleshed, with full and perfectly rounded breasts, slender hips, a scant blond pubic brush. Though she stood with her feet together, the insides of her thighs did not quite meet. She was inspecting Foxx while he looked at her. Joyce's eyes swept from his thickly muscled shoulders down the broad expanse of his chest and muscle-corded belly to his upthrust erection. She smiled sensuously but still made no move to touch him. Foxx began to feel like a prize bull or stallion in a show ring, being inspected for points.

"Do I pass?" he asked, half joking, half irritated.

"Oh, yes. With very high marks, Foxx."

"Shall I blow out the light?" He indicated the new Aladdin mantel lamp that stood on the dresser.

"Let's leave it on, if you don't mind."

Joyce moved across the small space that separated them and pressed up to Foxx. At the same time she parted her thighs to let his erection slide between them and squeezed her legs tightly together. She ran her palms up Foxx's sides, pulled his head toward her, and offered her parted lips. Foxx crushed Joyce to him, flattening the mounds of her breasts against his chest.

While their lips clung and their tongues entwined, she twisted her body slowly in his embrace, scraping the tips of her breasts against the coarse hair on his chest, contracting and slackening the muscles in her thighs. Foxx felt as though a huge hand was tugging and squeezing at his erection. He grew impatient to be inside her, and took a half step backward, trying to pull her to the bed.

Joyce broke their kiss and whispered, "No. Not quite yet, Foxx. Please."

Before Foxx could answer, her full lips thrust pouting against his, and opened to suck his tongue back into her mouth.

Many women had made many requests of Foxx, and he had always tried to respond. He stopped moving backward and began moving his hips slowly while Joyce continued to twist and writhe in his arms as she rubbed her crotch along the swollen fleshy cylinder she held between her tightly pressed thighs. The muscles that were squeezing Foxx began to quiver. He tightened his arms around Joyce's slender body, but she twisted her head to break their embrace. Her face was tense when he gazed at her, the small firm mounds of her breasts heaving, her nostrils flared.

"Now!" she gasped. "The bed!"

Foxx lifted her and whirled around. Joyce broke from his arms and toppled backward. She dropped the short distance with an athlete's sure control, a flash of stretching arms and legs that spread wide as she was falling. She landed in the center of the wide bed with each hand grasping an ankle, pulling her legs apart and stretching them straight; her torso a thicker column between two triangles formed by her joined legs and arms, spread-eagled, ready to take him in.

Foxx reached her with a single short step. Joyce's eyes were wide open and glistening in the lamplight, her full lips pulled back over shining teeth in a gasp of anticipation.

"Hurry!" she urged. "Go in as hard as you can!"

Foxx did not need her urging. He buried himself between her spraddled thighs in a single swift thrust. Joyce whimpered as he lunged, his hips thwacking against her thighs. Foxx felt her body begin to shake under his as he rose and plunged again, rose and plunged. The total vulnerability with which Joyce of-

fered herself and the depth of his penetration
brought him quickly to a new excitement.

Her muscles tightened as Foxx kept driving in with
swift hard thrusts. Her hips were gyrating beneath
him now, in twisting rolling movements timed to
meet his strokes.

Between gusting sighs, Joyce gasped, "Oh, Foxx!
Keep that up! Just a little bit longer—a little longer—a little—oh, hard now, now, now, now!"

Foxx was almost as ready as Joyce, but he kept control. Again and again he drove into her until she
clasped her hands over her mouth to smother the
scream that burst from her throat. Foxx let himself
go in one last downward lunge. Then he held himself, buried deeper than he'd ever thought possible,
while he shook and drained and felt Joyce's heaving
body relax in a succession of convulsive quivers until
she lay quietly beneath him. Then he fell forward,
relaxed and spent.

For a while neither of them spoke. Joyce broke the
silence with a satisfied sigh. "I'm glad I changed my
mind about you, Foxx."

"I didn't even know you'd made it up."

"I almost did. That first time I saw you, I thought
you'd be the kind of man who wouldn't enjoy doing
things a woman might want him to do. Or object to
them, things like that crazy position that makes me
feel so good. Some men are that way, you know."

"Not me. I want a woman to have her pleasure,
too." He stirred and started to move, but Joyce held
him with a sudden surprisingly strong grasping of her
arms and legs.

"And I like right now," she said. "I like to feel you
in me even when you're soft. But you're almost as big
soft as some men are when they're hard."

Foxx felt her begin to squeeze him with the sheath
of her inner muscles. He said, "I won't stay soft long
if you keep that up."

"That's what I hoped you'd say." Joyce speeded the tempo of her squeezes. "It's early. The whole night's ahead of us. I intend to enjoy it—and for you to enjoy it, too."

CHAPTER 15

Foxx woke at his usual time, fully alert. He stretched and started to get up, but on second thought lay back after lighting a stogie. In spite of the strenuous night, he felt rested. He'd left Joyce's room less than two hours ago, wearing only his pants, carrying his boots and other garments, and hurried down the deserted corridor to his own bed. He lay quietly for a few minutes, recalling the night and listening to the quiet. The shrilling of a locomotive whistle in the C&K yards shattered the stillness and intruded on his recollections. Foxx swore to himself and reached for the bourbon bottle. He took a swallow and leaned back on the pillows to plan his day.

Early morning, the time when most people were still abed, had long been Foxx's favorite time to think and plan. His sleeping habits were formed when Foxx was young. Before the buffalo hunters on the northern Kansas prairie had taken him back to his own people from the Comanches he'd acquired the Indian habit of waking at first daylight. Later, his struggles to readjust to white man's ways had showed Foxx that he needed more schooling than the bits and pieces his mother had taught him before he'd become a Comanche prisoner. To pay for his belated education, Foxx had worked for three years as the night attendant at a livery stable while attending school all day. He'd discovered during those years that he could function quite well on four or five hours sleep each night.

By the time Foxx had reviewed the scanty facts he'd been able to learn about the Becker brothers, and had summoned up a mental image of the stockpens and their surroundings, he'd smoked another stogie and had a second drink. The windows of his room were bright with the strange pale whiteness that spreads over the earth for a few brief minutes just before the sun appears. He threw back the blanket that had kept him warm in the cool night that late summer brings to Nevada's high desert plateaus. For just a few seconds, Foxx's nostrils were filled with the ghost of Joyce's perfume before the cool air of the room dissipated the faint haunting scent.

Dressed in the Levi jeans, denim shirt, and sturdy walrus-hide boots that he considered his field outfit, Foxx sat down to check his guns. He broke the forty-four Smith and Wesson American and turned its muzzle up to let the shells drop into his hand, then peered down the breech through the muzzle and found the bore shining clean. The cylinder pawl was free of dirt that might cause it to hang, and the tip of the firing pin shone intact through the hole on the frame's face.

Satisfied, Foxx reloaded and replaced the revolver in its holster. Then he put the House Colt through the same scrutiny. He took the Colt's soft leather boot holster from his valise, rolled up the leg of his jeans, and secured the weapon in place. Even though there would be enough men with him when the Beckers arrived, Foxx felt better with his backup gun in its place. When he rolled down the leg of his jeans the slight bulge made by the Colt's cloverleaf cylinder

was so slight that a casual observer would not notice
it.

Strapping on his gunbelt, Foxx took his Borsalino
from the dresser and went downstairs. The sun was
already showing above the peaked roofs of the two
big warehouses that stood beside the C&K yards.
There was no passenger train due for the next hour,
so Foxx walked to the depot lunchroom, where he
had a quick breakfast. His second cup of coffee warm-
ing his stomach, he walked along the right of way to
the stockpens.

Although the accidents of upbringing and geogra-
phy had kept him from service in the war, Foxx was
no armchair strategist. He knew that the advantage in
a fight or confrontation belonged to the side which
augmented courage with surprise and knowledge of
the field.

There was only one building at the C&K stockpens,
and it was small, Foxx saw when he reached the
cattle-loading area, a quarter mile from the yards.
The building was a little six-by-six-foot shanty that
provided shelter in bad weather where the railroad's
livestock agent could retreat to make out his waybills
and settle accounts with the shippers. The shanty
stood beside the loading chute at one end of the pens,
which were actually a series of small corrals surrounding a larger center corral. Aside from the dubious
protection the fences offered, the shanty was the only
place of concealment and shelter.

Foxx spent the better part of an hour walking
around the pens, studying the approaches to them.
There was no cover in any direction. The land to the
south, between the railroad tracks and the river,
nearly a mile distant, was treeless and without any
rock formation bigger than a pebble. Judging from
the condition of the ground, Foxx could tell that
most of the herds driven to the pens approached

along the equally coverless strip between the tracks and the river.

When he was satisfied that he'd learned all he could about the area, Foxx walked back to the depot and found Bob Scott.

"I guess everything's as ready as it'll ever be," Scott greeted Foxx. "Your man from the division's gone across the street to have breakfast; the other two will be here any minute. The rifles are right there"—he jerked his thumb at the cluster of Winchesters leaning in the corner—"and we've got more ammunition than I hope we're going to need. If there's anything else you've thought about, we've still got about an hour to get it."

"There's one more thing. But you didn't say anything about Rose Becker. She's safe and being watched, I guess?"

"She is. And if it's just the same to you, I'd like to forget her. She's a real mean one, Foxx."

"Like all her kin, I guess. Now then, Bob, that other job I mentioned. I didn't think about it until I went out a while ago and looked at the stockpens. I'd like to have the yard dinky run a cattle car up the siding and spot it right at the far end of the pens."

"If bullets start flying, that's not going to give the man in it much protection," Scott pointed out.

"It's not aimed to. It's just a place where he can hide until the time's ripe."

"Sounds like you've worked up a scheme."

"Pretty much of one. Soon as the men get here, I'll lay it all out, if you can wait until then."

"I'm not at all anxious, Foxx. I'll go have my clerk tell the dinkyman about that cattle car."

When his small force was assembled a few minutes later, Foxx explained why the Becker brothers had to be captured. The two yardmen from Elko, Calkins and Barnes, knew the brothers by reputation, and Foxx's man from Carlin, Matt Grey, had heard part of their history. Then Foxx launched into an explanation of his plan.

"We're not going out to gun anybody down," he warned. "If we do our jobs right and surprise the Beckers, nobody's going to get hurt. We might not even have to fire a shot. If it comes to shooting, we'll all be in the same boat. But there won't be, unless they shoot first. If they do, you men shoot to kill, because they'll be trying to kill you. Everybody understand that?"

All four of the men nodded. Foxx went on, "Bob, you and Barnes and Calkins are going to be hid in the agent's shanty, and you two take your lead from Bob. Now, there's going to be a cattle car at the end of the stockpens. I don't imagine the Beckers will pay much attention to it, just an empty on the north siding. I'll be inside the cattle car." He turned to Grey. "Matt, I recall you as being a pretty good rifle shot. I hope you've kept your eye in."

"I have, chief," Grey replied. "Matter of fact, I didn't know what was up when I got your wire to report here, so I brought along my pet Spencer, just in case." He indicated the Winchesters in the corner of the office. "They're good guns, but I'm more used to the Spencer. I'll shoot better with it."

"Use it, then," Foxx told him. "You'll be hiding under the cattle car, Matt. The Beckers have only got two ways to come in with their horse herd. They'll either drive up from the south, or they'll be coming along that strip between the tracks and the river, from the east. As soon as they get past the pens, I'll belly-crawl along the corral and get in back of 'em. Matt, you climb up on top of the car and take a bead on any one of the horses that one of the Beckers is riding. If they start shooting when I call for 'em to give up, you bring down that horse. Not the man, mind you. The horse."

Grey nodded. "I follow you, chief. The horse drops

and that stirs up a ruckus with the herd and takes
their minds off of you."

"That's how it ought to work," Foxx agreed. "Bob,
when you men in the shanty hear me hail the Beckers, you come out and string yourselves along the corral fence. Cover the Beckers, shoot if they shoot first.
Everybody got that?"

"What about the Beckers' horse herd?" Calkins
asked. "Won't them mustangs panic and bolt if
there's shooting?"

"Forget about the horse herd," Foxx replied. "If it
breaks up, let it. You be thinking about those Becker
boys. Now, I don't look for anything to start until
about noon, maybe a little bit before that. It was
about noon yesterday when I was at their trail camp,
and they were out trying to put the herd back together then. They might've brought them partway up
last night, they might not've started until this morning. But my guess is they'll be showing up here by
noontime at the latest."

Foxx sat on the floor of the cattle car, puffing at a
freshly lighted stogie. He looked through the open
slats past the corner of the stockpens, surveying the
trails by which the Beckers and their horse herd
would arrive. Both to the south and east the noon
sun glared at a deserted landscape.

Waiting for a fight to start, Foxx thought, is a hell
of a lot tougher on a man's nerves than the fight itself.

Breakfast had been a long time ago, and there was
a gnawing in Foxx's belly that reminded him the
other men waiting would be feeling hungry, too.
Hungry men waiting for a fight to start got edgier
than those who had full stomachs.

Foxx considered sending the men down to the depot one at a time to let them get something to eat at
the lunch counter. He turned the idea around and

looked at it from the top, bottom, and each side before deciding to wait a little bit longer.

*Unless the Beckers couldn't put their herd back to-
gether and went back home,* Foxx thought, *they
ought to be getting here just about now.*

If I figured everything out right, Foxx told himself
sourly. He stood up and looked again at the vacant
landscape to the south and east. In both directions
the horizon was devoid of moving figures. To the
south, the portion of the land he could see stretched
in a gentle slope down to a series of straggling ridges
that marked the river's flow at spring flood stage. To
the east the strip between the tracks and stream was
equally empty.

Foxx slipped through the slitted door on the blind
side of the cattle car and squatted down. Matt Grey
sat with his legs stretched in front of him, his back
propped on the flange of a wheel. His Spencer car-
bine lay across his knees.

"Any sign of 'em yet?" Grey asked Foxx.

"Not hair nor hide. Crawl up into the car, will you,
Matt, and keep watch while I go check up on the others? Whistle if you see anything."

"Sure." Grey crawled from beneath the car and
stretched. "You think they might not be going to get
here today?"

"It's too early to guess. We'll just keep waiting."

Foxx ducked along the right of way, using the
scanty cover provided by the corral's fences, to the
livestock agent's shanty. He went inside. The little
shack was crowded with three men in it, and his arrival packed it from wall to wall.

"I guess you're wondering what's holding up the
Beckers," he said. "Well, not any more than I am."

"We're getting pretty hungry," Barnes replied. To
Foxx, his voice seemed edgy. Barnes asked, "How
about me or Calkins going down to the lunchroom
and bringing back some sandwiches?"

Bob Scott caught Foxx's eye and nodded almost imperceptibly. Foxx said, "I guess we can spare one of you long enough to do that. A lone man hiking along the right of way wouldn't spook the Beckers, if they should get here and see you. Go ahead. And tell the lunchroom manager the grub's on the C&K."

Scott told Barnes, "Hurry it up, though. If that bunch is going to show up at all today, they'll be pulling in pretty soon." After Barnes left, Scott asked Foxx, "What do we do if they don't show up?"

"I'm still thinking about that, Bob. We'll wait, for now. It's about all we can do. When Barnes gets back, send a few sandwiches up to Matt and me, will you?"

Making his way back to the cattle car, Foxx found Grey standing, peering through the slats. He said, "Not a damn thing stirring, nor man or beast or bird."

"No use stewing about it, Matt. If they get here, they'll be here. If they don't, they won't. Anyhow, there's some food on the way. Waiting'll go easier with full bellies."

Time did not seem to pass easier after he'd eaten, but Foxx was worried about the effect the prolonged waiting was having on his men. Grey was a professional, he reminded himself, no need to worry about him. But Bob Scott and Barnes and Calkins weren't used to the strain of anticipating a fight during a long wait. Waiting made them nervous, and nervous men are unpredictable when a showdown comes.

In Foxx's mind the conviction was growing that he'd misjudged the amount of time the Beckers would have to spend rounding up the scattered mustang herd. He went over the schedule he'd worked out. Yesterday at noon, the brothers had been gone from their Pine Canyon camp for perhaps six hours. To sunset was another six. The mustangs would be tired after having bolted, the Beckers' horses tired from the chase. That meant a rest, a half day or a full day. And they'd still move slower than usual, he thought. The more he mulled over the timing, the more certain Foxx's conviction that he'd set up his trap a day too early.

"But I'd sure like to make certain," he muttered under his breath. "Except there's no way to make sure unless I ride out to scout, and then I'd risk running into them. Now, if I was just up on top of a mountain, where I could see all around—"

Foxx stopped short. Into his mind there'd come the echo of Joyce Kilpatrick saying to him, "You get a wonderful view of everything. In country like this you can see for miles all around you, even without going very high."

Foxx shook his head at the idea of him up in a balloon. But—the thought nagged at him—it'd sure be a way to scout. Maybe the only way.

For the next few minutes Foxx paced the floor of the cattle car, facing up to the problem. He took out his watch and snapped the case open; three o'clock, an hour away from the balloon ascension. Ten minutes to get to town and hire a hack, half an hour to get to the Humboldt Sulphur Hotel. Leave Matt Grey in charge here. If the Beckers hadn't arrived by now, the chances were good they wouldn't make it before tomorrow. And anything—well, almost anything—beat sitting on your ass waiting.

Foxx dropped to the ground outside the cattle car and called to Grey, "Matt! You take charge here. I just got an idea. If the Beckers don't show up in the next hour or so, you and the others go back to town, and we'll try again tomorrow."

"But, chief, if they—"

"Never mind any buts, Matt. Just do what I say!"

Foxx hurried along the right of way toward town. He wasn't looking forward to what was ahead, but it was the only thing he could think of, the only way to make sure. He'd feel like a fool if the Beckers did show up, with him up in the balloon, nothing under his feet but empty air. But he'd done a lot of other things he hadn't enjoyed and they hadn't been as bad in the doing as they'd looked to be as long as he'd put them off. He crossed the right of way to Railroad Avenue and began looking for a hack.

By the time Foxx got out of the hired carriage at the Humboldt Sulphur Hotel, he could face the idea of a balloon flight without worrying. The first thing he saw was the balloon itself. The big globular bag, sewed together from segments of red, white, and blue silk, had a tapering snout descending from its bottom. The balloon swayed gently in the light northwesterly wind. A crowd of several hundred had gathered in the turfed area between the hotel's three sprawling frame buildings. Foxx pushed his way through the chattering spectators until he was stopped by a rope barrier that kept a circle clear around the balloon. When he tried to duck under the rope, one of the three Elko policemen patrolling the cleared space rushed over.

"Back of the rope, mister!" the officer ordered. "Nobody's allowed to get closer than this!"

"I've got to talk to Miss—to Madam Asuza," Foxx said, taking out his wallet. He flipped it open to show the badge pinned to the inside flap. "Foxx. Chief of detectives for the C&K."

"Oh, well," the policeman touched his helmet. "If it's on official business—"

"It is," Foxx snapped. He was looking at Jocye. She was bending over the square wicker basket that hung by ropes from the net of cordage that enclosed the balloon bag. The basket stood a foot or so off the ground, Foxx saw. Heavy ropes tied to sandbags extended from two of its corners. Joyce had her back to him.

"You go on, Mr. Foxx," the policeman said.

Foxx stepped up beside Joyce and touched her

shoulder. She turned, saw Foxx, and her eyes lighted up.

"Foxx! You did get here!"

"Looks that way, doesn't it?" He looked at the crowd and at the wizened silver-haired man who had just raised his head above the side of the basket. He asked Joyce, "Can we talk in private for a minute?"

"Why—" Foxx's abrupt manner brought a frown flickering over her face. "I suppose so. I've got about ten minutes before I go up. But let me introduce you to Cap, first. Cap, this is Foxx. I told you how helpful he's been."

Cap extended a thin bony hand over the basket rim. "Pleased to meet you, Foxx." He said to Joyce, "Another five minutes or so and it'll be ready."

"So will I," Joyce said. "I want to talk to Foxx for a minute before I get in the basket, though."

She drew Foxx aside, between the basket and the first row of spectators crowding against the rope barrier. "Is something wrong, Foxx?" she asked.

"No. At least, not anything I can cure." Foxx hesitated before making the plunge. "I've got to ask you something first, before I tell you the rest of it. You said your balloon floats the way the wind's blowing. Question is, how far? And what do you do about getting back?"

Joyce stared at him with a question in her eyes, but let the question remain unasked. "Why—it'll sail southeast today. I don't know how far, but I'll be able to tell when I get up in the air. And as for getting back, Cap follows the balloon in a wagon that we've rented. I've got rockets in the basket to signal him with, if he doesn't find me before dark. Then I help him load the bag, after we get all the hot air out of it, and we come back to town."

Foxx took a deep breath. "Does that offer you made me of a ballon ride still stand?"

"Of course it does. But what about keeping one foot on the ground?"

"Just forget I ever said that. You'll take me along, then?"

"If you're sure you want to go up. I'd love to have you go with me, Foxx! And you'll enjoy it, as soon as you get used to the idea that it's perfectly safe."

"It's a deal, then. What do I need to do to get ready?"

Joyce looked at his well-washed Levi jeans and denim shirt. "Not a thing. Unless you want to leave your hat and gun here. Or you can put them in the basket; there are boxes in there where we keep the things I need for an ascension."

"I'll do that, then." Foxx looked past Joyce at the swaying bag of the balloon and made himself hold to his decision. "I guess I'm ready whenever you are."

"We'll have to talk to Cap a minute first. He'll want to adjust the ballast if you're going up with me."

Cap was standing beside the balloon. He showed no surprise when Joyce announced that she'd be taking Foxx up with her. Foxx thought, *I guess I'm not the first one she's given a ride to.*

Cap asked Foxx, "How much do you weigh?" He looked at Foxx appraisingly. "Hundred seventy, hundred seventy-five, I'd guess."

"Close enough," Foxx nodded.

Cap lifted several of the small canvas bags that hung around the edge of the basket and took a number of them off. He said to Joyce, "Well, whenever you're ready."

Joyce put her hands on the basket rim and vaulted lightly over the side. She motioned to Foxx, who levered himself up and in with quite a bit less grace. Joyce took Foxx's hat off and indicated with her fingers that he should unbuckle his gunbelt. She placed them in one of the long boxes that stood on two sides of the basket. Then she stepped up on one of the boxes and unclasped her cloak. The long red velvet garment dropped rustling to her feet. Foxx blinked. Joyce, clad only in clinging silk tights, was holding her arms out from her shoulders as though she would like to embrace the crowd of spectators.

Cap now held a megaphone in his hand. He raised it and began addressing the crowd as he walked slowly around the basket. Foxx could hear only a few scattered words. Cap was facing the crowd and turning from side to side as he moved.

"Ladies and gents!" Foxx heard Cap say, ". . . present Madam Asuza, the world-famous . . . in death-defying acrobatic feats . . . invite your attention . . . high in the air . . . and now, Madam Asuza!"

Joyce bowed to the crowd and stepped off the box. She moved to one corner of the basket, Cap to the other. They nodded and simultaneously pulled free the slipknots anchoring the balloon to its restraining sandbags.

Foxx was not conscious for a few minutes that the balloon was rising. He blinked as the upturned faces of the spectators seemed to diminish in size. Then the basket rocked gently as Joyce moved to his side.

"Well," she smiled, "it's not such a shock to get both your feet off the ground, is it, Foxx?"

For the first time Foxx looked over the rim of the basket, directly down. He saw the ground receding and gulped hard. Then he clenched his teeth. Between them he replied, "No. Not as bad as I thought it'd be. Worse, maybe, but not as bad."

Joyce was busy lowering a rope over the basket rim. "You sit on the box on that side," she told Foxx. "This only lasts a few minutes. But don't come over to this side of the basket, or it'll tilt. I'll be right back."

Foxx was not listening attentively. He was gripping

the rim of the basket while he lowered himself to the box Joyce had indicated. He felt the basket sway gently, and looked up. Joyce was gone, and the balloon was still gaining altitude. He blinked, not quite believing what he saw. He was quite alone in the basket.

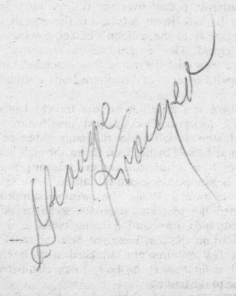

CHAPTER 16

For a moment Foxx stared, then he remembered what Joyce had said, that he was to stay seated. Cautiously, he peered over the rim. A dozen feet below him he saw Joyce, sitting on the bar of a trapeze hanging from the balloon's basket, waving a hand at the crowd. The balloon came to an abrupt halt, and Foxx now saw the ropes that extended tautly from opposite corners to heavy ringbolts anchored in the turf.

Joyce was standing on the trapeze bar now. She dived forward. Foxx gasped involuntarily, though he'd seen aerialists do the same thing before. She caught herself by her feet, thrust through loops in the ropes from which the trapeze was suspended. Then she began swinging pendulumlike, twisting her body as she swung. When the twisting stopped, she regained her seat and started a series of skin-the-cat, handstands, one-hand hanging twists, and other gyrations on the bar. Foxx got over the shock after the first few minutes and watched with interest until, with a final sweeping bow, Joyce clambered up the rope to the basket.

"How'd you like it?" she asked.

"Fine. After the first few minutes. Why didn't you tell me you did stunts like that?"

"There wasn't much reason, was there? It just never did come up, I suppose." She'd been hauling up the trapeze; now she moved over to the corner of the basket and pulled the end of one of the restraining ropes, then hurried across to release the other. Foxx didn't realize until he looked down and saw the ground diminishing again that they were now floating free and slowly gaining altitude.

Joyce said, "Suppose you tell me what made you change your mind, Foxx? About coming up with me."

In as few words as possible, Foxx sketched the misdeeds of the Beckers. He didn't mention the visit paid him by Rose or Ma Becker, and he interrupted himself from time to time to look back somewhat apprehensively. Each time he looked the Humboldt Sulphur Hotel and the buildings of Elko had shrunk in size a little more. He wound up, "So I figured the best way to scout the country and maybe find where the Becker boys are now was to take you up on your invitation."

Joyce shook her head. "You're the damnedest man, Foxx! You swear you'll never get more than one of your feet off the ground, but here you are, as comfortable as if you were in an easy chair."

"Maybe I don't feel as easy as I look," Foxx confessed. "But I generally manage to do whatever I've got to." He looked at the ground slipping by below, and then back at Elko, and guessed that they'd already covered as much ground as he'd been able to in the better part of a half day on horseback. He asked Joyce, "How far will this thing travel before it comes down?"

"That depends on how long I keep the burner going."

"Burner?"

Joyce showed Foxx the charcoal burner, suspended in the bag's tapering snout, just over their heads. He'd been so interested in looking down that he hadn't taken time before now to look up.

"As long as I add more charcoal now and then, we'll stay up. I usually let the burner go out as soon as I'm far enough from where the show started to keep a crowd from following Cap when he comes after me. If I want to go higher, I can drop ballast. But as long as the burner's going, we'll stay up."

"Suppose you want to go down and land?"

"I just pour a little water on the burner. When I'm landing, there's a spill panel that I can open to let the hot air out all at once, to keep the bag from dragging. Do you want to go higher? If you do, I can put on more charcoal. We're already beginning to drop a little bit. Look."

Foxx looked over the side. It seemed to him the ground was as far away as ever. He said, "This ought to be high enough. I can see a pretty fair slice of country right where we are now." He leaned back and lighted a stogie. For the first time, he felt relaxed. Ballooning wasn't so bad, Foxx concluded, and it sure covered ground quicker than a horse could.

"Are we going in the right direction?" Joyce asked.

"As close as I can tell, we are."

Foxx looked back. He could still see the Humboldt Sulphur Hotel, but it was a huddle of matchboxes now, and the buildings of Elko even smaller. He asked Joyce, "How far do you figure we are from town by now?"

She looked at Elko. "Fifteen or twenty miles. Why?"

"We'll need to go another fifteen or twenty. Are we going to be high enough to make it?" He looked ahead and recognized the long valley up which he'd ridden to Elko on his way back. He pointed. "There's the place I want to see."

"Twenty miles, I'd guess," Joyce said. "We'll be all right. Why don't you just sit back now and let go of the basket and enjoy the ride and the scenery down below?"

Foxx grinned sheepishly. He hadn't realized he'd been gripping the basket rim with both hands. He told Joyce, "I'm having a fine time. And the scenery I like to watch best is right here in the basket with me." He started to get up and join her on the seat across the basket.

"Oh, don't, Foxx!" she cautioned. "If we both sit on the same side—and I think you've got more than sitting down on your mind—we'll unbalance the basket and might start to spin. That's dangerous."

Foxx quickly settled back where he'd been sitting. He went back to watching the ground. He was getting used to the new looking-down angle by now, and ground contours as well as landmarks were becoming recognizable. The sun was nearing the horizon, and lengthening shadows on the ground made recognition easier. After they'd floated for what Foxx judged was eight miles or so he was sure he could see ahead of them the wide valley in which Pine Canyon was located. He began to wonder about getting back to Elko from such a distance.

"You said something about Cap coming after you in a wagon when you land. How the devil does he find you?" he asked Joyce.

"Why, he knows the direction the wind's taken the balloon. And there're rockets in that box you're sitting on. I wait a while after I land and fire one to guide him. I have to send up two or three sometimes, but Cap's been working with balloons a long time. He hasn't failed to find me yet."

Foxx glanced over the basket's rim. They were very close to the valley now. He could see halfway down

the far slope, cut with gullies and canyons. He tried
to locate Pine Canyon, but couldn't identify it among
so many. The balloon continued its steady progress,
and the valley floor became visible. Foxx saw the
dark blob he recognized as the isolated scrub pine.
He was just turning to point it out to Joyce when he
glimpsed movement. Looking again, he saw two men
on horseback galloping down the canyon. A few moments later, he could see why. They were hurrying to
meet a third rider who was hazing several mustangs
ahead of him.

"That's the Beckers!" he exclaimed. "It's got to be!
I didn't put much store in this scheme, but by God,
it's worked!"

"Are you sure?" Joyce asked. "We can go lower if
you want to."

"It stands to reason there wouldn't be but one
bunch of three men driving mustangs in this iden-
tical same place. But if it's not too much trouble,
maybe I could see better if we went down a little bit
more."

Joyce took a spouted can out of the box under the
seat, poured water into her cupped hand, and
splashed it on the burner. Foxx watched her briefly,
then as the balloon began to lose altitude, turned his
attention back to the three riders.

They'd seen the balloon by now. Their faces were
turned up, watching its progress. The big bag kept
dropping lower, and soon Foxx could see their features distinctly.

"It's them, all right," he said with satisfaction. "I
just saw the youngest one that time in San Francisco
I told you about, but those fellows look so much alike
you could pick 'em for brothers at midnight in a coal
cellar!"

As the balloon swept slowly over them, Foxx could
tell by their gestures that they'd begun arguing.
Eddie, the only one he could identify positively, was

pointing at the balloon and haranguing his brothers. Belatedly, Foxx realized that recognition had worked two ways. The brothers were drawing rifles from their saddle scabbards. They began shooting at the balloon.

"Damn me for a constipated jackass!" Foxx exclaimed. "They recognized me, too! Joyce, how fast can you get this thing up higher?"

Slugs began whistling through the basket as the Beckers found the range. One came through the wicker floor, barely missing Joyce. She looked up at the big silk bag and frowned.

"If they put a lot of holes in that bag, we might not be able to stay up much longer," she warned Foxx.

"Can I do something to help?" he asked.

"Drop some ballast. There's a cord with a button on it at the bottom of each ballast bag. Pull the cord to let the sand out. Don't dump too many bags, or we'll rise too high and get out of control."

Foxx hurried to follow her instructions. He dumped two bags of sand, and a bullet tore through another, emptying it. The balloon began gaining altitude, but they were still low enough for the Beckers' rifle shots to reach them.

Suddenly a slug pinged as it hit the burner. Glowing coals dropped onto the floor of the wicker basket. Wherever a coal fell, the varnish on the reeds bubbled and started to smoke.

Her voice controlled, but tense with urgency, Joyce said, "We've got to put out those coals or the basket will catch fire!"

Foxx tried to stamp out the glowing coals, but his bootsoles only forced the embers into the spaces between the reeds. Heedless of the rifle bullets that kept singing through the flimsy basket and disregarding the pain that the glowing charcoal inflicted on his fingers, Foxx dug the coals out one at a time and tossed them over the side. Kneeling on the basket floor, he rubbed the burning reeds with his fingertips to extinguish what remained of the flames.

"Look out, Foxx!" Joyce shouted.

Foxx looked up, but could see no danger. Joyce stood at one side of the basket, fumbling with a sack of ballast. Foxx started to stand up, but before he could move, a scraping bumping noise sounded under his knees. The basket tilted violently, and Foxx was almost thrown out. Joyce stretched out an arm. Foxx managed to grab it. .

With Joyce's hand steadying him, Foxx stood erect and looked over the side. The balloon was at ground level and the basket was being dragged over the rocky soil. Somehow Joyce managed to pull the cords on two more bags of ballast. Slowly the basket straightened up. The bumping and scraping stopped.

"I thought we'd be high enough to miss that bluff, but the wind pushed us into it," Joyce explained. "We'll have to put more charcoal in the heater fast. Look ahead."

Foxx looked. A second cliff, its face almost vertical, loomed about a mile in front of them. He looked back. The rim of the bluff they'd scraped now hid them from the Beckers, but Foxx knew the brothers would not give up their pursuit. Joyce was busy adding pieces of charcoal to the burner and coaxing them to light. The balloon was beginning to rise slowly again.

"Can we get up high enough so we won't smash into that cliff ahead?" Foxx asked.

"I hope so. We're not really in very good shape though. They shot too many holes in the bag. I'm afraid some of them have started to rip, and when that happens, more hot air escapes than the burner can generate. We might not be able to go very much farther."

Fox had been studying the face of the cliff, now just a few hundred feet ahead. It appeared to him the balloon would clear the steep rise and its sheer face would present a real barrier to their pursuers. The Beckers would be forced to leave their horses at its base and climb the rise on foot. At the least it was a position he could defend.

"Can you land on top of that cliff?" Foxx asked.

Joyce looked quickly at the cliff. They were high enough now to see that the ground beyond its crest was almost tableflat. She nodded. "Yes. I can bring us down there without any trouble. It's a good high place, too. Cap can see our signal a long way off."

"Go on and land then," he told her. "I can hold off the Becker boys as long as my shells hold out. Words ain't going to stop them three. The only thing they understand is hot lead. And if we expect to leave here alive, I'll just have to give 'em a bellyful!"

CHAPTER 17

As the balloon sailed closer to the cliff, it seemed to Foxx that they were gaining speed. The top of the ridge was still bathed in sunlight, but the shelf was darkening and he could see that sunset's shadow would soon be creeping over the top as well.

Joyce lifted the metal burner pan out of its bracket and tossed the burning coals over the side. She said, "I'm going to use the spill panel now. It lets the hot air out in one big puff, and you'll have to jump out as soon as we touch ground and grab the basket so the bag won't drag it."

"Can I help you get out?"

"Don't worry about me, Foxx. I'm used to jumping out in a hurry. I'll be right by you, pulling my weight."

Suddenly the top of the cliff was below them. Joyce grabbed the end of a dangling rope and yanked it. Above them Foxx heard a great *whoosh* and the basket dropped like a stone.

Everything happened at once after that. The silk bag sagged and the bottom of the basket grated and began to lean. Foxx jumped out; Joyce vaulted over the rim of the basket to join him.

They grabbed the wicker sides and held it reasonably still while the collapsing balloon gave a final pulsing tug. Then with a sad *sshhh* of escaping hot air the bag crumpled to the ground, spreading itself flat. A few wrinkles and humps showed where pockets of hot air had been trapped, but these began to flatten out almost at once.

"That wasn't bad, was it?" Joyce smiled. She held out her hand. Foxx took it. Then when her fingers tightened around his, he winced involuntarily at the stabbing pain that followed the pressure. Joyce asked, "What's the matter?"

"My hand. I reckon I burned it a mite when I was putting out them coals after that rifle slug hit the burner. We been too busy for me to pay any attention to it before now."

Joyce turned Foxx's hands up. The left didn't look too bad; it had a few puffed blisters in the palm, and the tips of its fingers were bright pink. His right hand was another matter. It was badly blistered, and some of the bigger ones had burst, exposing the soft, tender layer of underskin.

"That looks terrible!" she exclaimed. "And I don't have a thing to put on it. Does it hurt a lot?"

"Not till I try to use it. Hell, don't worry about it. We got to start thinking about them three Beckers. Now that we've had to stop, they'll be catching up with us pretty soon."

With one mind they turned and walked to the rim. Joyce said, "Speak of the devil—"

Foxx could see the three riders just coming into sight over the edge of the shelf where the balloon had first touched ground. They had a little more than a mile to cover to reach the base of the cliff where he and Joyce were standing. He watched them for a moment, then went back to the basket and climbed inside.

Joyce followed him to the basket. She asked, "Can I do something to help, Foxx?"

"Not unless you can conjure me up a rifle from someplace."

He was rummaging in the storage box where he'd put his gunbelt. The jarring of the basket had jumbled up the contents of the box; Foxx had to dig the revolver out of an untidy heap of spare rope and empty ballast bags and signal rockets. He found it at last and started to buckle it on. His burned right hand was too sore for him to manipulate the buckle.

Joyce saw the trouble he was having and climbed into the basket to help him. She asked, "If your hand's too badly hurt to buckle this belt on, how're you going to handle a gun?"

"I can do good enough shooting left-handed, at close range. And them fellows can't ride up the face of this cliff, Joyce. I can move along the rim a lot faster'n they can move while they're climbing up."

"It's going to be dark soon. The sun's already down. How can you see to aim?"

"I'll manage. Now you stay back from the rim, where you'll be safe from stray bullets. Ain't there something you oughta be doing with the ballon before it gets too dark to see?"

"I can fold it up, unless you need me to help you."

Foxx waited until Joyce started to pull at the edges of the collapsed bag, stretching it out in preparation for folding it, then walked back toward the edge of the cliff. Before he got close enough to it to see the Beckers or to be seen by them, he dropped to the ground and belly-crawled to the rim.

Picking a spot where his silhouetted head would blend with a large boulder, he looked over the shelf. The Beckers were coming fast; they were now only a few hundred yards from the base of the cliff. The light was fading rapidly, but when Foxx stretched out flat and looked down along the face of the cliff, he could see that in spite of its almost vertical rise a man could scale it without too much difficulty.

There was one spot, only a short distance from his present position, where a rock overhang thrust out from the rim like a huge eyebrow. The overhang extended for perhaps twenty feet. It was the best place he saw for a lone man with a crippled gun-hand to station himself. Anyone climbing the face would have to expose himself before crawling over the rim.

Foxx rolled to the center of the overhang and lay quietly, careful to keep his head back from the edge of the rock formation. He heard the hoofbeats of the Beckers' ponies thud up the the base of the cliff and stop. Then Eddie Becker's voice reached his ears clearly.

"You sure this is the right place, Stud?"

"I'm certain of it. I seen the balloon go down and kept us in a straight line, all right. They're not more'n ten feet one side or the other of where we are now."

Stud's voice was heavier and rougher than Eddie's. Foxx filed its tone and timbre in his mind. Then Cal Becker spoke.

"Well, hell, if you're all that certain, let's go on up and take care of 'em!"

"Don't be in a hurry, Cal," Stud said. "We'll get rid of that damn railroad detective, sure. Not the woman, though, not till after we've all had a go at fucking her."

"If we're going to do it, let's start!" Eddie urged. "We sit on our butts down here too long, they'll get away!"

"Don't get roiled up!" Stud snapped. "Soon as I figure out the best way to handle things, we'll go after 'em."

For a moment the trio was silent. Foxx heard only

the pawing and snorting of their horses. Then Stud spoke again.

"Cal, you're better with a rifle than me or Eddie, and the two of us oughta be able to take care of that Foxx son of a bitch. You stay down here by the horses and cover us while we're climbing up. I don't want him potshotting at us while we're going up there."

"Wait a minute, now!" Cal protested. "If I stay down here and miss out on the fun, I oughta get first go at the woman."

"Like hell!" Eddie snorted. "Me and Stud's going to do the hard work. You get her when we've had our turns."

"Shut up, both of you!" Stud rasped. "Here's how we'll settle things. Cal, you got as good a chance to get Foxx as me or Eddie. Whoever kills him gets the woman first. I'd say that's a fair and square way to do it."

"Suits me," Cal agreed. "Just don't you forget, if I shoot Foxx from down here, you save the woman for me."

"Don't worry." There was a creaking of saddle leather and a crunching of booted feet on gravel, then Stud went on, "All right, Eddie. We better get a move on. The light's going awful damn fast. Let's start climbing."

Foxx decided the Beckers wouldn't be paying much attention to the rim of the cliff for a few moments and risked peering over the edge. The shadows at the base of the cliff had deepened almost to the darkness of night, but he could still see them dimly. Cal Becker was taking his rifle out of its saddle scabbard. Stud and Eddie were walking along the base of the rise, looking for the best place to start their climb. Foxx pulled his head back and started thinking.

He'd counted on the three Beckers staying together. The one with the rifle at the base of the cliff shifted the odds to favor the brothers. Now he'd have no

chance to pick the climbers off at close range, and he
had no illusions about his ability to match his left-
hand revolver shooting with Cal's rifle. There was
still enough light for shooting, and silhouetted
against the sky he'd be cold meat for a rifle shot before he could get off an aimed shot at Cal.

*If that one with the rifle wasn't there, I'd be all
right,* Foxx thought. *But unless he's blind as a bat—"*

A chord twanged in Foxx's memory. The sound of
boots scraping and loose rocks falling below him
added urgency to his thinking. Foxx crawfished away
from the rim and ran crouching to where Joyce was
sitting on the edge of the big square of silk into
which she'd folded the balloon.

"I heard most of what they said," she told Foxx.
"Let's be sensible now. With your right hand in the
shape it is, you can't take on three-to-one odds. It'll
be pitch dark in a few minutes. Let's get out of here
and find a place to hide!"

"No, Joyce. All they'd do is wait till daylight and
root us out. Now I can take care of 'em, if we handle
things right."

"I don't see how."

"You will in a minute. Go get me about four of
them rockets outa the ballon basket."

Joyce wasted no time asking questions, but vaulted
into the basket and took the rockets out of the storage
box.

"I'll need some help now," Foxx told her as he
took the rockets and started for the rim. Joyce levered
herself out of the basket and followed him.

Before their movements could be seen from the
shelf below, Foxx dropped to the ground. Without
waiting to be told, Joyce did the same thing.
Crawling up to the edge of the smooth solid rock
ledge that formed the overhang, Foxx used his un-
burned left hand to begin clawing gravel from the dirt
at the edge of the rock. After looking at him with a

puzzled frown for a moment, Joyce helped. Foxx let her continue digging while he took two stogies from his pocket, and lighted them with a match shielded in his cupped hands.

"Hold these," Foxx said. He handed the glowing cigars to Joyce. "It'll take a minute for me to set up these rockets. If the cigars start to go out, puff on 'em to keep 'em lit."

Using the sides of the rockets as though they were scrapers, Foxx pushed the the pebbles ahead of him and wormed up to the lip of the overhang.

He risked one quick look over the edge. Cal Becker was standing beside the horses, his eyes moving along the rim of the cliff. He missed seeing Foxx by not more than two or three seconds. Below him Foxx could hear Stud and Eddie climbing up the face. In the murky dimness almost as dark as night now, he was unable to see them, but the noises they made sounded too close for comfort.

Foxx made four piles of the pebbles, as close to the rim as possible. Then he worked a rocket into each of the gravel piles, the round bodies of the rockets forming their own launching cradles. He aimed the noses at the spot where Cal Becker stood beside the horses. The rockets set, he motioned for Joyce to join him.

"Keep one stogie and give me the other one," he told her when she'd crawled up beside him. "When I give the signal, you set off them two, and I'll take care of the other ones. Try to get yours going about the same time as mine."

Joyce nodded that she'd understood and handed him one of the glowing stogies. She warned him, "Roll away from those rockets fast, Foxx, or you'll get singed."

They stretched out side by side. Foxx made a circle in the dimness with the glowing tip of the stogie he held, and touched it to the fuse of the first rocket. As soon as the fuse spat at him, he touched the coal to the second. Together he and Joyce rolled away from the streams of spewing sparks.

On the shelf below, Cal Becker began shooting when he saw the first sparks from the rockets, but Joyce and Foxx were well back from the rim. Within seconds the sparks became trails of bright flame as the rockets streaked from their pebble cradles and shot toward the shelf.

Foxx stood up. Using his slit fingers to shield his eyes, he watched the rockets land. All of them hit within a yard or so of Cal and the horses. A moment after the rockets buried their noses in the earth the sizzling fuses ignited their main charges. Great balls of red and yellow and white shot up from their bases, lighting the landscape with a brilliance that shamed the noonday sun.

With frightened snorts the horses reared, then bolted. Cal Becker was staring into the blazing rocket exhausts, too surprised to shield his eyes from the blinding glare. By the time Cal recovered from the shock of the rocketry, Foxx had his S&W out of its holster.

Holding the revolver in his left hand, Foxx rested the long barrel of the weapon on his right forearm and took careful aim at Cal. The slug turned Cal halfway around. He let the rifle clatter to the ground as he fell.

Foxx dropped flat just as Stud Becker's head showed above the rim. At such close range Foxx's left-hand shooting was accurate enough. The bullet from the pistol smashed into the oldest Becker's face. Stud dropped and Foxx heard his body tumbling to the shelf.

Eddie popped up from the rim a yard to one side of the spot where Stud had been. Foxx wheeled and snapshotted. The slug hit Eddie's shoulder and knocked him off his precarious perch. Foxx heard the last of the brothers start rolling down the cliff-face to

the accompaniment of falling rocks and sliding
gravel.

Stepping up to the rim Foxx looked down at the
shelf. The rockets were sputtering, but still gave off
enough light for him to see clearly. Cal Becker was
trying to sit up, but a bloodstain spreading at his
waistline told Foxx that his low shot had shattered
Cal's hip.

Bending forward Foxx saw Eddie getting to his
feet, one arm flopping uselessly. A few yards away
Stud Becker's body lay still, face down. The horses
were nowhere in sight.

Joyce came up, coughing, in time to get a glimpse
of the shelf just before the last rocket sputtered out.
Between gasps she asked. "What are we going to do
with them, Foxx?"

"Not a damn thing. The two that's left can bandage each other up, but I don't imagine they'll move
much, not without horses." Then, as Joyce broke into
another coughing fit, he asked, "What's the matter?
You swallow wrong?"

"It's your damned cigar, Foxx!" she gasped. "I got
so excited that I inhaled just before we touched off
the rockets. What on earth is in those things?"

"Nothing but good strong tobacco, the kind the
Italian fishermen in San Francisco like. I picked up
the taste from them."

Joyce shook her head. Then she asked, "Are you
sure those two down there will be all right?"

"Stop worrying about 'em. They'll live to face a
judge. Let 'em do for theirselves till Cap gets here
with the wagon, then I'll corral 'em to take into
Elko."

"It's going to be a long wait."

"I figured that. He won't make it here much before
daylight, I'd imagine."

Joyce looked at him, a slow smile parting her full
lips. "No. But we'll be comfortable enough. There

are sandwiches and a bottle of wine in the basket. And that bag makes a nice soft mattress."

It was Foxx's turn to smile. He put an arm around Joyce and they started walking slowly back to the balloon.

DELL'S ACTION-PACKED WESTERNS

Selected Titles

- [ ] **THE RELUCTANT PARTNER**
  by John Durham $1.50 (17770-7)
- [ ] **BOUGHT WITH A GUN** by Luke Short $1.50 (10744-5)
- [ ] **THE MAN FROM TUCSON**
  by Claude Cassady $1.50 (16940-2)
- [ ] **BOUNTY GUNS** by Luke Short $1.50 (10758-X)
- [ ] **DOUBLE-BARRELLED LAW**
  by D. L. Wrinkle $1.50 (11773-9)
- [ ] **THE KIOWA PLAINS** by Frank Ketchum $1.50 (14809-X)
- [ ] **LONG WAY TO TEXAS** by Lee McElroy $1.50 (14639-9)
- [ ] **LOCO** by Lee Hoffman $1.50 (14901-0)
- [ ] **LONG LIGHTNING** by Norman A. Fox $1.50 (14943-6)
- [ ] **DIL DIES HARD** by Kelly P. Gast $1.50 (12008-X)
- [ ] **BUCKSKIN MAN** by Tom W. Blackburn $1.50 (10976-0)
- [ ] **SHOWDOWN AT SNAKEGRASS JUNCTION**
  by Gary McCarthy $1.50 (18278-6)
- [ ] **SHORT GRASS** by Tom W. Blackburn $1.50 (17980-7)
- [ ] **DERBY MAN** by Gary McCarthy $1.50 (13297-5)
- [ ] **YANQUI** by Tom W. Blackburn $1.25 (19879-8)

At your local bookstore or use this handy coupon for ordering:

Dell **DELL BOOKS**
P.O. BOX 1000, PINEBROOK, N.J. 07058

Please send me the books I have checked above. I am enclosing $ _____
(please add 75¢ per copy to cover postage and handling). Send check or money
order—no cash or C.O.D.'s. Please allow up to 8 weeks for shipment.

Mr/Mrs/Miss _____

Address _____

City _____State/Zip _____

Another bestseller from the world's master storyteller

The Top of the Hill

IRWIN SHAW

author of *Rich Man, Poor Man* and *Beggarman, Thief*

He feared nothing...wanted everything. Every thrill. Every danger. Every woman.

"Pure entertainment. Full of excitement."—*N.Y. Daily News*
"You can taste the stale air in the office and the frostbite on your fingertips, smell the wood in his fireplace and the perfume scent behind his mistresses' ears."—*Houston Chronicle*

A Dell Book $2.95 (18976-4)

At your local bookstore or use this handy coupon for ordering:

Dell	**DELL BOOKS** THE TOP OF THE HILL $2.95 (18976-4)
	P.O. BOX 1000, PINEBROOK, N.J. 07058

Please send me the above title. I am enclosing $_____
(please add 75¢ per copy to cover postage and handling). Send check or money order—no cash or C.O.D.'s. Please allow up to 8 weeks for shipment.

Mr/Mrs/Miss_____

Address_____

City_____ State/Zip_____

The

The third chapter in the triumphant saga that began with *The Immigrants* and continued with *Second Generation*

Establishment

The Lavettes—a special breed. A powerful and passionate clan. Swept up in the McCarthy witch-hunts, struggling to help a new-born Israel survive, they would be caught up in a turbulent saga of war, money and politics. All would fulfill their magnificent destinies as their lives became a stunning portrait of their times.

A Dell Book   (12296-1) $3.25

Howard Fast

At your local bookstore or use this handy coupon for ordering:

Dell	**DELL BOOKS** P.O. BOX 1000, PINEBROOK, N.J. 07058	THE ESTABLISHMENT	(12296-1) $3.25

Please send me the above title. I am enclosing $ _____
(please add 75¢ per copy to cover postage and handling). Send check or money order—no cash or C.O.D.'s. Please allow up to 8 weeks for shipment.

Mr/Mrs/Miss _____

Address _____

City _____ State/Zip _____

ARENA

NORMAN BOGNER

"Another *Godfather!* It has virtually everything!"—*Abilene Reporter-News*

The spectacular new novel by the bestselling author of *Seventh Avenue*

Four families escaped the Nazi nightmare with dreams that could only come true in America.
For Alec Stone, the dream was a boxing arena.
For Sam West, it was a Catskill resort—a refuge for his beautiful, speechless daughter, Lenore.
For Victor Conte, it meant establishing a west-coast talent agency.
And for Paul Salica, it meant a lasting committment to another family—the Mafia.
But to young, gifted Jonathan Stone, no dream was big enough. Obsessed by love for Lenore, he would risk all they won—again and again.

A Dell Book   (10369-X) $3.25

At your local bookstore or use this handy coupon for ordering:

Dell	**DELL BOOKS** ARENA (10369-X) $3.25
	P.O. BOX 1000, PINEBROOK, N.J. 07058

Please send me the above title. I am enclosing $_____
(please add 75¢ per copy to cover postage and handling). Send check or money order—no cash or C.O.D.'s. Please allow up to 8 weeks for shipment.

Mr/Mrs/Miss_____

Address_____

City_____ State/Zip_____

BESTSELLERS

☐ **TOP OF THE HILL** by Irwin Shaw $2.95 (18976-4)
☐ **THE ESTABLISHMENT** by Howard Fast........$3.25 (12296-1)
☐ **SHOGUN** by James Clavell $3.50 (17800-2)
☐ **LOVING** by Danielle Steel $2.75 (14684-4)
☐ **THE POWERS THAT BE**
  by David Halberstam $3.50 (16997-6)
☐ **THE SETTLERS** by William Stuart Long $2.95 (15923-7)
☐ **TINSEL** by William Goldman $2.75 (18735-4)
☐ **THE ENGLISH HEIRESS** by Roberta Gellis....$2.50 (12141-8)
☐ **THE LURE** by Felice Picano $2.75 (15081-7)
☐ **SEAFLAME** by Valerie Vayle $2.75 (17693-X)
☐ **PARLOR GAMES** by Robert Marasco $2.50 (17059-1)
☐ **THE BRAVE AND THE FREE**
  by Leslie Waller $2.50 (10915-9)
☐ **ARENA** by Norman Bogner $3.25 (10369-X)
☐ **COMES THE BLIND FURY** by John Saul $2.75 (11428-4)
☐ **RICH MAN, POOR MAN** by Irwin Shaw $2.95 (17424-4)
☐ **TAI-PAN** by James Clavell $3.25 (18462-2)
☐ **THE IMMIGRANTS** by Howard Fast $2.95 (14175-3)
☐ **BEGGARMAN, THIEF** by Irwin Shaw $2.75 (10701-6)

At your local bookstore or use this handy coupon for ordering:

Dell **DELL BOOKS**
P.O. BOX 1000, PINEBROOK, N.J. 07058

Please send me the books I have checked above. I am enclosing $ _____
(please add ·75¢ per copy to cover postage and handling). Send check or money
order—no cash or C.O.D.'s. Please allow up to 8 weeks for shipment.

Mr/Mrs/Miss _____

Address _____

City _____ State/Zip _____